Acknowledgements

Thanks to friends and relatives
for the help provided in
producing this work.

Kodoma ga san nin imasu
Ross, Nicholas and Charlotte

This is the second 'Steele' novel.
The first is 'I Have To Get It
Right'

This novel is entirely a work of fiction.
The names, characters and incidents portrayed in it
are the work of the author's imagination. Any resemblance
to actual persons, living or dead, events or localities is
entirely coincidental.

Copyright © David L Atkinson November 2011

First published by CompletelyNovel.com 4th November 2011

ISBN – 13 9781849142182
ISBN – 10 1849142181

Printed by Lightning Source UK Ltd

All rights reserved. No part of this publication may be reproduced, stored in a retrieval system, or transmitted, in any form or by any means, electronic, mechanical photocopying, recording or otherwise, without the prior permission of the publishers

This book is sold subject to the condition that it shall not, by way of trade or otherwise, be lent, re-sold, hired out or otherwise circulated without the publisher's prior consent in any form of binding or cover other than that in which it is published and without a similar condition including this condition being imposed on the subsequent purchaser.

The 51st State

Chapter 1

Walking home from the pub is not pleasurable anymore, from two main points of view. First, the alcohol offered in the pub is no longer the smooth, hoppy beverage, that was not particularly high in alcohol content, but that fuelled the social interaction between friends, neighbours, colleagues and lovers. No! Now it is sweet, fizzy and unnecessarily strong fuelling nothing other than drunkenness, violence and noise. The kids' party has grown up and moved into the pub! The second is the rubbish in the streets. It is almost impossible to put a foot down without stepping on or kicking some detritus from a fast food shop or coffee emporium. I suppose that comment is as much about the way we teach our children to clear up after themselves as it is on the way that food is presented for purchase. Much of this, of course is not biodegradable and firms based in the USA sponsor all of it and there of course is the root of the problems we now have.

During World War 2 our leader, Winston Churchill, was desperately eager to persuade the Americans to take their share of responsibility for world peace, when he coined the phrase 'special relationship', which he then applied to the relationship between the UK and the US. It worked then and probably has its basis further back in history but whatever, since Churchill's time, it has been used as a guilt-provoking tool to engineer what are actually false relationships between the two nations. Thatcher used the term, as did Gordon Brown when we were descending into recession in 2008 –09. Whenever it has been used there has been some source of stress in the country. The problems growing out of the 'special relationship' have all come back to bite us!

These were the thoughts running through my head as I picked my way through the litter on my way home. I have been walking this route home for almost five years and the volume of rubbish has increased noticeably in that time. To make matters worse a car veered towards the pavement I was walking on and a hand shot out of the window and a half full carton of coffee was thrown towards me. The car was full of drunken youths. A metaphor for the things I had been thinking moments before!

Once I got to bed I went on thinking along similar lines. Sleep wouldn't come! Our little country had been so influential round the world for centuries, but what were we now? An American annexe! The media perpetuated the situation both overtly and covertly, if that's possible. Americanisms are infecting every aspect of our lives and therefore our English culture. The major crisis came when the so-called 'credit crunch' of 2008 hit the world. It is probably an oversimplification but political decisions made by Mrs Thatcher and subsequent US Presidents making borrowing easy have fuelled this sad situation. How ludicrous to allow people to borrow seven times their salary! How can they pay it back? Of course when it all went wrong US sneezed and we all caught a cold as the saying goes, but did we learn our lessons? No!

It is very difficult when the youth and young adults in the country worship everything American; our culture has no chance when we are so easily persuaded by the shiny baubles of their culture. Surely our roots should be with Europe if we are to maintain our independence.

The really worrying situations that have arisen over the freeing of the Lockabie Bomber and the oil well disaster in the Gulf of Mexico give greater cause for concern. MPs from the Scottish and English Parliaments summoned to face US senate hearings! The Scots made me proud with a downright refusal as they should have, but what did we do in England? We actually considered going and then the Foreign Secretary decided he couldn't because he was on holiday. No balls! We are not answerable to the American Government and never should even have considered the possibility of going.

So what does it all mean? Has our government sold us down the river? Are we really to be the 51st State of the Union or are we already there? It may not be the case formally but at times there seems that there is nothing to choose between us.

What can be done about it? Are these just the ravings of a slightly drunk old-fashioned Englishman? Is this all from my imagination? I spent some time pondering what actions ordinary people could take to turn the tide away from the west and back to the glories of our own culture. I must have fallen asleep because the next thing I knew the sun was up. I still felt disquieted by the thoughts of the previous evening and wondered what was to be gained by thinking in that way.

It could have been set off by the chat in the pub last night or maybe the visit to this country of a senate delegation looking into the amalgamation of the US and UK banking systems. Surely that would lead to one currency and therefore one country – hence the 51st state!

My job is to chase money and 'fix' problems. That's what I do I fix problems and get paid for it. Anonymously! How I do the fixing depends on the nature of the problem. I have developed a number of skills both legitimate and not so!

Some developed during a very interesting three weeks learning to be a Bodyguard at Officer Training School. Also my time at university in the gun, sailing and climbing cubs. How I got a 2:1 in Maths I don't know.

  The courage to take action! I was 16 when my Uncle was killed. I had been a regular visitor, spending holidays. He was an interesting man and I enjoyed his company. But one afternoon someone walked into his house and robbed him of his wallet and frightened him so much he had a stroke. He fell against an armchair, which was then pushed against the gas fire and it started to smoulder. My Uncle died of smoke inhalation. To cut a long story short I found out who he was and went after him with my Dad's golf club – the driver! I was young and got away with a non-custodial sentence, but the dye was cast.

  My name is Patrick A Steele and I am an independent agent in the fight against unfairness. Sounds grand but I suppose the best way that I can explain it is that I am a sort of 21st Century Robin Hood acting both independently and occasionally with the Gurentai. They are a sub group of the Japanese Yakuza, a mafia style organisation that spent centuries making money from the proceeds of crime and its' members were Robin's merry men of centuries ago who used the proceeds purloined by the Yakuza to help the needy in society. They are still in existence as are the Yakuza, although the relationship is not at all close, and I had been recruited by one of their number one Takuo Sumisu. I did a job on the Italian Mafia a few months ago and have hit various targets since saving ordinary people from extortion and other crimes. This was a rather different situation because I want the backing from the Gurentai to help me overcome what is possibly even too grand a proposition for them. This is an international situation that could be nothing more than a figment of my imagination but I would stake my life that I am correct.

All of this before breakfast! I would text Sumisu and set up a meeting. My first action was to work out. I put on my jogging suit and set off to my private facility. It is a mile or so from my apartment and has been well furnished by the payments I received into my Swiss bank account from previous work done for the Gurentai. It is well appointed too. A lot of equipment that you would find in a standard gym including a sauna; a dojo where I practise my aikido with the help of a local black belt - Vince Thompson has been installed; there is also a garage for my three vehicles; and, a limited domestic facility.

The cars are my toys. I have a Jaguar XF Portfolio with a 3 litre V6 diesel engine in dark blue; a silver Mercedes SLK Class Grand Edition with the SLK 350 six cylinder BlueEfficiency engine with stunning acceleration and suite of extras; and, finally a black Renault Espace 2011Grand Dynamique for anonymous work. They are always prepared for use thanks to Bill Fordyce who keeps my second place in full working order. He and his wife Stacey look after all my domestic needs. They are a middle aged couple who are in semi retirement and wanted part time work to see them through to full retirement; both are in their mid-fifties and have been with me for three years. Absolutely reliable and trustworthy and they have become quite close friends. They don't ask too much about what I do and I allow them to share the gym facilities. I turn a blind eye to them allowing their family to use my facilities as long as it is limited. Stacey keeps my apartment in immaculate condition but also deals with mail when I am not around, secretarial work really, but with attitude! I am indebted to both of them.

My Aikido sensei, Vince, is retired and comes to my dojo everyday for an hour in the morning and we have an intense 45 minutes work out that includes meditation techniques as well as attack and defence. He thinks I am at black belt level, which I should be with all the individual tuition I have received, but can't understand my reticence in not wanting to go to an assessment event. It is too public and that doesn't fit with what I do. Even so I am still no match for Sumisu!

I texted him to request a meeting at a local and anonymous hotel. As usual I would have to wait without any real sense of when he would get back to me so rather than waste time I thought about the argument in favour of this assignment in which I want to involve the venerable gentleman! Essentially I would provide him with the evidence as I see it and then outline the visit from the American politicians and the possible consequences. As far as I am concerned incontrovertible!

After a rather frustrating day I received a rather terse message,

"The Hilton, Leeds tomorrow at 13:00"

As always I arrived slightly before time but not early enough to get there before Sumisu san. He was in the lobby enjoying his usual cup of Ocha – green tea.

"Konnichiwa Patrick san. O genki desuka?" he smiled.

I bowed as did he, but mine was lower because he is senior to me.

"Konichiwa Sumisu san. O genki desu, Arigahto. Anatawa?" I replied.

The revered gentleman smiled benignly,

"I am well thank you Patrick, and your accent is improving!" this with a slight chuckle.

We've come a long way since our first 'job' although proprieties still need to be observed.

"Why have you requested this meeting Patrick san?" he inquired politely.

"It's a long story going back many years Sumisu san. Suffice it to say that it began when our government was almost begging support from the US towards the end of WW2 to the present day when the latest bill to be discussed in Parliament is the Gun Bill which is intended to give our citizens the right to own hand guns!" I stated.

"We are no more than an addition to the USA. Our culture is disappearing and I feel we need to stop the rot. Even our language has been hijacked; you can't get served without the obligatory 'have a nice day'"
     I finished my torrent of words feeling somewhat flustered and slightly embarrassed.

"Patrick san you are obviously very upset about the situation in your country. This is a situation that has been progressing for seventy years why do you think we Gurentai could have any influence on such an embedded condition?" he responded.

This is the point where I had to get my sales pitch correct or I was on my own.

"It centres on US foreign policy that has been in force for many years. It brought about the fall of Saddam Hussein, the Ayatollahs in Iraq and the division of Afghanistan. If the UK with its dwindling world influence becomes an annexe of the US the tide of their influence will eventually sweep over Europe and will continue to spread eastwards. Japan will not be immune in years to come. The signs are there already. Just look at your department stores Sumisu san. Where are the cultural reminders in the goods for sale? They have gone and been replaced by cheap rubbish driven by the vulgar music business from America." I had been talking really rapidly and when I finished there was a pause that seemed to go on forever.

"I understand your argument Patrick san. What I am prepared to do is to discuss this at a higher level. It may be seen as too late for the UK in which case we won't be able to help. On the other hand your argument may be seen as totally correct and if this proves to be the case, you will have our full backing. However, I would imagine the answer will be somewhere in the middle of those two extremes and that is only because of the excellent work you have done for us in the past. I will contact you in a few days with the decision." He finished.

"Thanks Sumisu san." I said gratefully.

The remainder of the meeting was about the range and type of activities I might indulge in to turn the American tide. After an hour or so we took our leave of each other.

While I was 'cooling my heels' waiting for Sumisu to get back to me I started to think about my own plans if the Gurentai were not going to help.

At the Hilton we had discussed the types of long term action that would have the desired deep cleansing affects. There were various assassinations that would create a political storm but in some respects there were too many targets. I had the feeling that it would come to that in the end anyway when a suitable target had been identified and if all else failed. For now the disruption of things American in connection with our future is probably the route to take to establish some quick wins, which in turn may galvanise the apathetic masses to rise up and make themselves heard against the indomitable tide of US colonialism.

So the initial move would be to disturb the forthcoming visit of the US Finance group. There were some easy actions that could be taken. Initially to disrupt the travel plans from Heathrow and then, a little more ambitious, cause injury to one of the delegates. One thought that had crossed my mind was the abduction of one of the members of the Treasury department but that could well be too extreme and what would be gained? Probably very little because the government could slap a 'D' Notice on the media and stop publicity. The first two steps I have outlined would not be difficult to achieve and would certainly attract enough attention to raise the matter. Working on the principle that 'trouble comes in threes' there must be something else that would focus the attention on the reasons to be anti-US.

The first step, with or without the Gurentai, would be to carry out a little research into the US delegations travel plans. I assumed that they would fly into Heathrow but something in the back of my mind was niggling me about that. I believe that Royalty, Senior Politicians and other notable personages tend to fly to a military establishment. There are a number close enough to London to be suitable and I would need to find out which one and be there before our visitors from across the pond. There are nine airports in and around London so it would not be easy to ascertain the date, location and time of arrival. Sumisu may be able to help with that through one of his many contacts.

The other issue, the 'accident' to one of the group may be a little trickier. I would have to get very close to the party, their hotel, or wherever they were being billeted. There will be massive security cordons round them from the moment they touch English soil to the moment they leave. Another job for the Gurentai! I was being very dependent on them and I had received no assertion from Sumisu that they would be involved in anyway whatsoever. So I would need travel arrangements and information as to where these Americans would be staying before I can even begin. I went to bed that night feeling fired up at the prospect of some action and frustrated that I would have to wait for the Gurentai before I can finalise my plans.

Chapter 2

The US party would be in the UK in a week and I still had heard nothing and was on the verge of texting Sumisu when he turned up at my annexe. He has a habit of doing that. I turned round during one of my slow one legged balance turns on my dojo and there he was!

"You have gained a greater level of self-control Patrick san." He smiled. "Good morning Patrick san!"

"Good morning Sumisu san," I said bowing low.

He indicated we should go into my living quarters. I led the way. Stacey Fordyce was cleaning up. When she saw us entering the living room, she got flustered and excused herself very rapidly. Sumisu smiled and bowed which made her even more embarrassed and she almost ran out of the kitchen into the gym! I would have to explain the correct procedure to greet my 'boss' and de-mystify him a little. I invited Sumisu to sit down and then offered green tea – ocha.

"Patrick san," Sumisu began, "my superiors have come to a decision and it is as I suspected. They concur with your assessment of the overall situation and feel that it may be too late for the UK but they also feel that the USA must be stopped before they have achieved world domination. They do see a further possibility that may protect UK sovereignty and that is closer links with some of the European countries, principally Germany and France, both powerful movers in their own right with similar problems as the UK although not as advanced. We are prepared to offer the full facilities we possess to help you achieve your aims acknowledging the fact that you may not be successful!"

That was a salutary warning in no uncertain terms but it wasn't something I didn't expect.

"Thank you Sumisu san and I would appreciate you expressing my gratitude to your principles. May I begin with two requests? It may seem indecent haste but the Americans will be here in a week's time and only for three days." I stated.

"Certainly Patrick san go ahead," he replied.

"Firstly, I require information about where they will arrive in the UK and the time as well as where they are to stay. Secondly, I would like some idea of their timetable while they are here?" I demanded.

"I will be back with you in a day with that information." He stated succinctly.

My eyebrows climbed up my forehead at the explicit nature of his reply.

"Do not be surprised Patrick san. We monitor major political situations as a matter of course!" he responded.

"Thank you Sumisu san. I will proceed with my plans." I said gratefully.

After another ten minutes chat, including an inquisition on how my Aikido was progressing, he left as quietly as he arrived.

Stacey appeared in the living room at the flat a few minutes after I had arrived and it was obvious that she was curious by her body language. I explained that Mr Sumisu was one of my employers and that he was from Japan and liked to follow the Japanese traditions.

"You mustn't worry Stacey. He will always bow to you, and will not shake hands. Just bow if you feel you can, he will not be offended!" I explained. "Oh, and Stacey, it might be wise to mention it to Bill. Sumisu has a habit of just appearing!"

She seemed happier now that she was 'in the know'.

I settled down to sketch out in my mind the actions that I am going to take. I will have little time to reconnoitre the situations and so I will have to travel fully 'tooled up'. I have developed a number of skills both legitimate and not so! Some of them gained from a very interesting three weeks learning to be a Bodyguard at Officer Training School. Also as a result of my time at university in the gun, sailing and climbing cubs! How I got a 2:1 in Maths I don't know. In my recent tasks for the Gurentai and before, I have acquired some pretty 'nifty' gear that I have come to rely upon.

There is a Glock concealment T-shirt with my Glock 17 fitting snugly into its pouch. I also have a 7'' bladed carbon steel Glock standard issue knife as used by the Austrian military, and a Swiss OM 50 Nemesis sniper rifle with replacement barrels detachable sight and silencer. The barrel lengths are 15 – 33 inches and used depending on the distance of the shot. There are also lots of other fancy things I have been furnished with by the Gurentai, including a spray that dissolves wire found in chain-link fences - that has come in useful more than once, as well as numerous other useful gadgets.

    I would have to take most of the kit with me. I had safe, locked cabinets let into the floor of the annexe at the back of the unit. They were checked by the police annually as was my gun licence, a situation that will be less strenuously policed if the new gun law comes into force. Damned Yanks! I put the equipment into the Mercedes M Class Grand Edition. Bill created special pockets in the vehicle to stow the various weapons in preparation for when I go 'hunting'. I also had quality luggage with false bottoms for some of the smaller tools that I use. The clothing I wear for secret surveillance is predominantly black including a black overall to mask ordinary street clothes for the purpose of quick change and eluding pursuit. Recently I have started to acquire weapons that are not detectable by security devices that are designed to pick up metals, including a Busse Stealth Hawk knife and a small automatic pistol with a magazine of similar bullets loaded into the handle. When you pull the trigger, a plastic spring drives the bolt/slide mechanism forward, pushing a bullet from the magazine into the chamber and firing it. It is made from some type of ceramic and was developed by the CIA and supplied by Sumisu and his pals. How they got hold of it I didn't ask!

    I am expecting that my sniper rifle will be used for the first task, which will be the disabling of their transport. They will have back up vehicles; it is only intended as an inconvenience and to flag up with the media that these people are in our country. For the second task I am unsure as to what I will use or where I will be acting but need to cause a minor physical injury, a broken bone, or concussion, enough to bring about temporary hospitalisation of one of their team. Then perhaps a third incident, if necessary, that will be geared toward attracting anti American feeling. That will very much depend on the reaction to the first two events! I have no doubt the CIA is going to be very cross with me, if they find out who I am so after the initial attacks life is going to be very much more interesting. The germ of an idea was coming to mind that involved exposing the CIA acting in our country. I had a picture in my head of a CIA operative on local TV admitting his role in the UK! That may take some organising but is not impossible.

That then of course would result in our own security services waking up and chasing me as well. Life may be a little tricky for a while! I have already set in motion negotiations to own a property on the continent, France being my optimum choice. I have holidayed in France many times and feel quite at home there. It could be that I will need to speed that deal up so that I have a bolthole.

Of course it would be ideal to have some support from our own security agencies, MI5 in particular. The problem there is that, if I am right, they will already be under the influence of the CIA and more of a hindrance than a help. On the other hand the domestic intelligence services of France and Germany may be coerced into giving some support. Or will they be frightened of the CIA shadow?

For now I would pack my gear, work out and wait for news. I did just that but with the added enjoyment of an hour in the local with my friends. It had its uses because I could maintain my cover of overseas account management explaining my intermittent absences. I'd even speculated that I may buy a property in France and they could borrow it for holidays. The money coming from this highflying job I do! In reality from my Swiss bank account with Micheloud & Cie that Sumisu keeps well topped up!

The following morning I went for my daily run finishing at the annexe. Vince came and we worked out especially hard, I wonder if he had a nudge from Sumisu to get me up to scratch! I didn't have long to wait when the phone rang. It was Sumisu with the information that I required.

The party were landing at London Biggin Hill airport. They would arrive at 2am on the morning of the 27th October. They were due to travel to a large private house/farm about 2 miles west of the airport. There are 4 negotiators each with their private secretary and bodyguards, a total of 20 people, mostly male! At a guess mostly CIA! A reclusive millionaire, with a penchant for security, owns the house where they are staying. They would remain in the country until midnight on Sunday. Their programme is to consist mainly of meetings to be held in the house where they are staying, however, they will travel into the City on Friday to visit the Prime Minister and attend a state dinner at the Palace travelling back to their billet at the end of the evening. There is some allowance of free time but not so much as to allow trips of any distance. The place where they are staying has ample grounds, tennis court, swimming pool and stables for their recreation.

So there it is my imposed itinerary! I have three days to get to Biggin, become familiar with the lie of the land and confirm my plans. There is also a need to find somewhere to stay. I'm sure there will be plenty of pubs and not a lot of trade at this time of year when the weather is turning towards winter's style. I'll set off on Monday morning and be there by mid-afternoon. Having researched a suitable hotel I've come up with The Fox and Hounds at Westerham Hill. A typically English hostelry offering me fine ales and good food, not gourmet, but most certainly wholesome and well presented. I rang them and booked a room from Monday evening until Sunday morning.

  Monday morning I set off and had a trouble free journey. The weather was dry but with some cloud cover and a threat of showers later, and the temperature was in the mid-fifties Fahrenheit around 12 degrees Celsius. The forecast was similar until the weekend and then a warm front moving up from the southwest would bring rain. Hopefully I wouldn't be working outside by the weekend! I arrived as planned and deposited my bag in the low ceilinged, beamed room. I walked into Westerham and had a look round as any tourist would before returning for my evening meal. The town is a pleasant and for the most part a dormitory for people who work in the city, it has to be said for the middle management range of people. Some of the houses are quite grand! I decided to go to bed quite early because of what I needed to achieve the following day and also over the days to come.

  The following morning, Tuesday, I took a drive to the airport and then travelled west towards the large farm estate, where our unwanted guests would be staying. I didn't even slow down because the hedges and trees surrounding the farm have cameras at every strategically important position and I've no doubt they will record every vehicle that passes as well as those that enter. There is also a private road to the property that is about 100metres long. There is no way I can approach the house without being seen. There are majestic, mature Lombardy poplar trees lining the approach road. As magnificent as these tall trees are, they provide very little cover because of the lack of growth low on the trunks. The route from the airport is rather tortuous involving a short journey northwest before turning back on itself and then approaching the estate from the east along a farm track. Travelling by road all of the way is an even further circumventing of the countryside round the estate. I'd imagine the vehicles used will be a fleet of black Range Rovers. I'd seen the type used by security services previously. Looking at the layout there was no way I can take out vehicles at the estate. The road they'll have to follow has a junction where they will turn and that is well wooded. That's where I will carry out my first assault.

   There is a stand of trees on the side of the carriageway opposite the road junction. The vehicles will slow to turn left into what is a narrow road, I'll let the front three go, and then take out the last two, I am assuming there will be 5 or 6 vehicles. Damaging the back two would mean they could not get support from the first vehicles which will allow me to get away with ease. I parked up at the side of the road I had targeted as my hide and had a look round spotting the best position for cover. It actually didn't take that long. The scrubby woodland provides considerable opportunities for concealment, and as it is bordering a country lane I can get the car back into the woods behind where I am going to be positioned, on a convenient track into a field just a little way along. That track ran through the woods parallel with the lane and came out into a farmyard that then accessed the main road back to Westerham. Very convenient - but I would still use my false number plates! The nights are closing in which will enable me to set up quite late, as it will be dark. I will use the sniper rifle, short barrel - two tyres and a bullet in the engine block for each vehicle. That should probably take less than ten seconds from first till last. The confusion in the vehicles would last for longer so I would be long gone before even the professionals of the CIA could react. I returned to my hostelry feeling quietly confident of success of the initial part of this action, the questionable strategy would be getting one of the delegates on his/her own to cause them damage. I could shoot them from a mile away but that is not the purpose of the exercise. The point is to disrupt American negotiations without engendering sympathy from the populace. An accident would be blamed on the delegate and not a third party.

      It was going to take some working out. The site of their lodgings had been chosen exceptionally well which is hardly surprising considering the combined intellect of the available security services. Its solitude and the number of guards, cameras and possibly even dogs would make my initial attack the closest I was going to get to the farm buildings as the plans are set in my head at the moment. The alternatives were the trip into the city on Friday and any unplanned sojourns into Westerham or the surrounding towns. What I couldn't do was sit around the estate entrances twiddling my thumbs until someone came out! The journey into London would be impossible to disrupt as would the time spent in the offices of state and the Palace. No it would have to be when one of the 'inmates' decided to go for a walk or a brief trip into Westerham but this was a weak plan. The germ of an idea came to me as I was thinking about how to carry out the second part of my plan. My thought processes are well served by my reflecting empathetically as to what life would be like for the Americans during the few days they will spend within the fortress that is this farm. There will be one particular time when the farm is going to be more vulnerable than for the remainder of the visit of the Americans, and that is on Friday. It may be that a planned piece of sabotage would work rather than targeting an individual.

I have enough experience to organise a fire in a barn or set up sabotage within the house and other living quarters. Friday would be relatively quiet until they returned because the security will be with the personnel who are more important than buildings in this case. In fact the more I thought about it the risk of discovery will be less than if I try causing an accident to one of their people. The course of action decided upon will have to be arrived at very soon, particularly if I required specialist equipment as time will be needed to acquire it.

As I sat eating a sumptuous beef and ale pie for my lunch I pondered all these ideas going through my head. I decided to hedge my bets and request some equipment from the Gurentai. Although getting a fire going may not require anything more than candles, balloons and a fuel source. Lighter fuel and aerosols are transportable and don't draw attention if purchasing them, nor do candles and balloons. I could be quite creative when I wanted to be! What I am going to do is request satellite observation of the estate from Sumisu. I feel that it is within his compass to provide that. I decided to ring him on his mobile when I left the pub on a shopping spree this afternoon. As far as the landlord is concerned he thinks I am here on business until the end of the week. I didn't tell him that, but he talked himself round to the reason for me being in his pub while I made non-committal grunts over a pint of his flat southern beer! Who am I to dissuade him from that position?

I took my time over the bitter coffee that had been served up, went to my room and put on a tie, shirt and jacket, and, looking very much like an accountant, set off to the supermarket and various hardware stores in the area to purchase the things I may need to create a suitable conflagration! I bought a packet of balloons from a newsagent, a travelling alarm clock from a hardware store along with batteries and lighter fuel from a tobacconists, and sugar from the supermarket. Why sugar? Well I saw my father liven up a dying coal fire with sugar on more than one occasion. Quite an effective accelerant! I also bought a reel of copper wire from a large diy store. I was ready to make a homemade incendiary device! My thoughts had almost totally turned from causing injury to an individual to a massive disruption of the visit. What better time but when the party are in London with their entourage? There will still be the owners and their people around but that should not present too much difficulty.

When I got back to my room I decided to wire up my device in preparation for Friday. The US party would arrive by 2am tomorrow morning and so I needed to get some rest this evening before my nightshift! It would also allow me to set up some of the equipment I would need later. The device I was constructing consisted of a battery operated clock, and a heating coil. The remainder was in the preparation of a source of fire created from the sugar, any materials available such as paper or textiles, for the heating coil to ignite. The balloons filled with lighter fluid were to enhance the conflagration they would spread the fire further and faster. I went as far as wiring the battery to the clock and completing the circuit with the coil. I tested it and after a couple of attempts I got the correct length of wire to ignite a piece of paper with the coil. Once this was achieved I knew that my device would work. A fire would have the immediate affect of getting everyone out of the farm in the middle of the night and create the confusion I was hoping for. I had no intention of hurting anyone but inconveniencing everyone. I then settled down to a few hours sleep. I set the alarm on my mobile phone for midnight so that I had plenty of time to get to the ambush point and yet feel rested.

    I didn't think that I would sleep but I must have done because I woke with a start when the alarm sounded. I quickly showered and dressed in my black clothes, collected my equipment for this particular task and left the room. The landlord had given me a door key to use if I was late back in the evening and there was a side door that led into the car park through a tiny foyer. I wasn't likely to bump into him and there were no other guests but I still did not want to be seen or noticed in anyway. I took my time and eased out of the Fox and Hounds and into my car very quietly. I drove the vehicle out of the car park and off eastwards towards my target without the benefit of headlights until I was out of the immediate vicinity of the pub. It only took a quarter of an hour to get to the airport and another five to attain my hiding place. I had kept a careful eye on my mirrors and made sure that when I turned off the lane and into the field I wasn't observed. I found the track through the woods, it resembled a rather foreboding tunnel entrance in the dark, and crept along it so that I was quite close to the farmyard through which I would make my escape. I turned off the engine and got out of the vehicle and stood very still for fully five minutes giving my eyes time to adjust to the darkness and also to flex my muscles. I don't think I took a breath in that time, although I must have to have survived! There wasn't a human noise that

I could identify. There were some wildlife noises as you might expect - rustlings and snufflings, but nothing human I was sure.

After a few more minutes I was satisfied that I could move safely and collected my Swiss snipers rifle with the short barrel and the tripod that I use to steady it and set off to the site I had selected for my shooting position. It is 01:30 and our guests are due to touch down in a few minutes. I am close enough to the airport to hear a plane landing and it wasn't long before the throaty drone of an aircraft approached in the distance. I probably had half an hour before there was any sign of the Yanks. The lights of an aeroplane were visible as pin pricks in the velvety night sky. I used the time to settle into a comfortable position and to ensure that I'd a good view of the road. I made myself as comfortable as possible and settled down to wait using my Aikido relaxation techniques to focus on my inner core and maintain my warmth and concentration.

I did not have long to wait. I didn't think that I would. No passport controls, baggage collection or customs to queue at for these guys! There were a number of vehicles travelling along the country road from Westerham in convoy and with all lights blazing like a rapidly moving luminous snake. I sighted the far side of the road with my night sight and regulated my breathing. The convoy would be here in a couple of minutes. I watched the cars manoeuvre round a bend in the road and slow as they approached the left turn they would make to go to the estate which was their destination. I watched as the lead vehicle turned and proceeded more slowly. There were five vehicles. So I let the first three go. They were no more than ten metres apart. I took aim at the radiator grill of the fourth vehicle and waited until they were almost fully turned before firing three times, once into the engine block from the side and into both offside tyres which deflated immediately. I was already firing into the radiator grill of the final vehicle and had blown its tyres before the fourth had ground to a halt. I was up and off through the trees, quickly but quietly before anyone had left either car. I went straight to my Mercedes put the rifle in the back and set off quietly through the woods towards the farm, no lights. The Blue Experience engine rumbled quietly as I crept through the unlit farm buildings and out on to the road about 50 yards from where the two damaged Range Rovers were stood. I glanced in my rear view mirror and saw a number of people making a very wary cordon round the wounded transport. I was tempted to stop and take a longer look, but common sense prevailed and I continued on my way.

It was almost 02:30 when I got back to the Fox and it was in total darkness. I entered as quietly as I'd left and went up to my room. I had no sleep in me with the adrenalin coursing through my veins. I lay gazing at the ceiling and pondering my next move. There was nothing to do but wait. I had a couple of days to track the movements of the inmates of the estate and prepare equipment for a fire on Friday. I may have the opportunity to hit one of them before Friday but I rather doubted it, they have been alerted now! So it will be down to Plan B to cause more disruption and ill will between the Americans and their hosts. One slight disappointment is the lack of feedback I will receive on this first action. It doesn't matter how old you are it is human nature to need feedback when you have performed a task. I was winding down and felt myself getting drowsy.

Chapter 3

I woke up as curious about the affect of my attack as I was when I was falling asleep last night. I showered and went down to breakfast where I chose the usual full English that meant I wouldn't eat again until dinner this evening. I had requested black pudding when the landlady had asked if there was anything I wanted in particular. She came good this morning! Delicious but I bet my arteries were screaming for mercy by the time I had finished!

I decided to leave my vehicle in the car park and stroll into Westerham. It is be a 5-mile round trip that I need to complete to keep fit after the huge meals that the landlady was serving up. It was also a salve to my conscience! Also I wanted to keep an ear open for any gossip or news that might have filtered through. There must be local people who work on the estate. People in small towns and villages talk! Knowledge is power!

I followed some footpath signs to the rather grandly named Royal Biggin Centre. It turned out to be a glass and steel constructed, modestly sized shopping centre containing small versions of high street stores, including, sadly, Starbuck's and MacDonald's. Having stuffed my face at the hotel I decided Starbuck's would benefit from my custom. Standing at the counter I gazed at the list of beverages available and shook my head. I must have spoken my wish for an ordinary cup of coffee aloud because I got a reply from a young girl smiling at me from behind the counter,

"Americano sir?" she sounded more bored than she looked.

"Yes please." I replied.

At that point she went into another set of options.

I interrupted her with a sigh, "Just a cup of coffee with semi-skimmed milk, no fully skimmed milk please."

    She duly obliged and when it came it was a good cup for almost £3! I carried the drink to a table that made it possible for me to watch the room and see out through the plate glass window into the shopping precinct. The coffee was at the usual superheated temperature and so was going to last me a while. Just as well I was becoming impatient and needed to stop and think about what my next actions will be. I had not been sat for much more than five minutes when I spotted a familiar body shape approaching through the increasing number of shoppers. Small, dapper in a navy three piece suit and walking steadily with short steps. Sumisu - and he is not alone! He was in the company of a rather tall girl wearing a silver grey business suit. She must have been at least 5'10" slim and with a striking inverted teardrop of a face. How does he always know where I am and where does he find these beautiful girls? I wish I had his luck!
    I went back to the counter and asked the barista, because that is the title given to the counter girls by Starbuck's, for two cups of Twinings green tea and took it back to my table where Sumisu was already sat with his companion.

"Good morning Patrick san" he said with a slight inclination of his head. "This is Naomi Kobayashi an associate of mine! She may be of assistance to us in the near future!"

"Good morning Sumisu san. Good morning Naomi san." I said.

She bowed and smiled politely but said nothing.

"What brings you by here this morning Sumisu san?" I inquired.

"I was going to ask how things were going Patrick san." He countered.

I spent a few minutes running through the previous day's actions and my plans for Friday.

"Yes a local garage was contacted to take away the damaged vehicles and two new vehicles have just arrived." He explained. "Your plan for Friday is good but very risky. Also Naomi san may be of great help when it comes to negotiations with the French and Germans. She is fluent in their languages as well as one or two others!" he stated.

We sat in silence for a few minutes. Each considering what alternatives there may be. I was watching the girl. As with all Aikido, except for me, she exuded an air of calm authority. She hadn't spoken, because she is shy or so I thought, but as I was to find out later that is far from the truth, more because she was in control and taking in her surroundings and undoubtedly me. I felt thoroughly assessed!

I glanced out at the passers-by and something caught my attention. A lone man was walking towards the coffee shop! It was the way he walked and how he was dressed that caught my attention. A big guy, around 6' 2" well built and sporting a crew cut. He was wearing a navy blazer over a white shirt and blue tie, pale blue trousers and black shoes. The guy walked into Starbuck's and ordered a caramel macchiata with extra vanilla and fully skimmed milk. The latter seemed pointless! What was interesting was the accent. Sumisu was watching my gaze.

"From one of the southern states I would say. Don't you think Patrick san?" smiled my mentor.

He stood and said,

"We will leave you to it Patrick san. Please be careful!"

With that they stood, bowed and left. I was always left with a feeling of inadequacy round this fellow, and on top of that there was now an equally enigmatic female to contend with!

It was almost as if he had read my thoughts! I was considering how I could damage this American fellow without getting spotted. I watched his back as I finished my coffee in a rush; at these prices I was leaving nothing! Naomi was not with him! What on earth! Anyway, I had no time to investigate, I decided to leave and wait outside in the main mall. There were enough people around now to cover my stealthy observations.

I found a bench about two outlets from the coffee shop and sat and observed the door using the newspaper I had just bought as cover. Suddenly I felt my hand being held gently and turned to see Naomi smiling at me.

"I thought it might aid your disguise if you were to have a companion!" she stated kissing me on the cheek. (I am in love already!)

"Thank you Naomi san. That is a good idea!" I replied beaming from ear to ear!

Suddenly this job was feeling much more interesting.
    It only took about 10 minutes before our American target stood and left the coffee shop. He headed towards our seat and passed, aiming towards the escalator leading down to the lower level. An idea sprang to mind. I got up quickly and headed after him holding on to Naomi. I knew that there was an emergency stop button on the side of the escalator at the top and bottom. I could see the moving staircase as I closed with the top and there was no one else on it. Buddy stepped on and started moving down. He was stepping down as well as moving with the treads. Perfect. He was gathering speed and was half way down when I hit the button and moved straight away. I heard the escalator screech to a halt and then a yell. I stepped on the spiral staircase the alternative way down to the ground floor, and descended glancing to my right. The American was in a mess at the foot of the staircase with a gathering crowd of people all trying to help and getting in each other's way. He tried to get up but fell back down. His face was bleeding where he had hit the metal treads and there was a spreading patch of blood on the pale blue trousers below his right knee. Someone had called an ambulance from

their mobile and they were bringing things out of the nearby shops to make him comfortable.

We stuck around until the ambulance arrived; joining with the crowd of onlookers, and watched them carry him into the ambulance. Naomi and I walked on to the exit of the shopping centre.

"I will leave you now Patrick san." She kissed me on the cheek again, I could get used to this!

"How will I find you? What are you going to do to help? Where are you staying?" I gabbled.

"So many questions!" her voice was quiet and clear like a mountain stream burbling over polished pebbles. "I will be in touch on Friday when you have finished at the estate."

With that she turned and glided away. It wasn't walking it was like poetry but so quick!

Serendipity - a propensity for making fortunate discoveries while looking for something unrelated. In other words this had been a 'happy accident' – but not for our Yank travelling towards the hospital at the moment. I believe I had achieved two of my original targets and there was a day and a half to gauge the reaction of the delegation. I decided to go out to the estate and observe the behaviours. The guy I had nobbled was obviously one of the guards, maybe even CIA, but there would be some reaction nevertheless!

The following day, Thursday, was a waiting day. I busied myself testing my heating coil, walking in the countryside and doing some clothes shopping using my ill-gotten gains. Eventually, I went to bed early and set the alarm for 05:00. It is my belief that the party would leave for London early as they had a very full day ahead. I wanted to get in there when the remaining staff is relaxing for a few hours before their duties resume much later in the day. Also I didn't want to harm any of our own people so the sabotage would take place during the day in as remote a position as possible to cause the maximum amount of property damage.

While I'd been shopping I had bought a small rucksack, for the purpose of carrying my various pieces of equipment to the residence. I would also take my Glock17 and knife but I wasn't planning any 'wet work'.

It was going to be very difficult to get in and out unobserved in broad day light but it was total anonymity I was hoping for. I had also bought a navy boiler suit and a baseball cap. I wanted to appear to be some kind of maintenance man if observed at all. There was nothing I could do at such short notice if I was pulled up and asked for any credentials. Speed and stealth were the keywords for the day.

I parked the Mercedes in the same place that I used when shooting at their cars. I then set off walking to the left along the country road away from the estate access road. It is a very quiet lane and so I didn't expect to see anyone or to come across any vehicles except for maybe a tractor or two. From an aerial view I had seen on the internet there was a small track leading off this lane into the estate at right angles to the access road. I intended to take this because it had a hedge about a metre high. It could be dangerous. If I was protecting the place I would have guards on all access roads irrespective of how big. On the other hand they were not guarding anything today!

It was still early and quite dark as I turned on to the track. There were no lights as yet. The party would not have left so guards would be still in position. I strolled very carefully and quietly doing my best to control the sound of each footstep. Dawn would break in about an hour and I wanted to be as close as possible to the outbuildings, of which there were several, before that happened.

The track had a ninety degree turn to my right then another to the left a few yards further on, at that point the track was lined with the Lombardy poplars on the right but the track proceeded straight forward towards the property. If there were going to be guards I felt that it would be on one of the two acute bends. I paused and squatted down in the lea of the hedge to listen. Having seen an aerial photograph of the property from the web I knew that this side of the estate was quite complex in that there was an access road, some rubbish and old machinery dumped which would make my approach that much easier. As I recall there are two long buildings on the right and the main house was on my left as I approached with the tennis courts further to the left. The buildings on the right were probably the stables. I have a fondness for animals particularly the huge, soft brown eyed horses that would be housed there and fire is a terrible stimulant to them. They would be traumatised if the conflagration approached the stable block.

The house itself was a rather plain two storey mock Georgian, brick built structure. There was a small porch with pillars supporting a canopy over the front door. Judging from Google Earth there was plenty of neatly trimmed grass around the front and rear of the house. There must be around 10 bedrooms in the main property and then there was what appeared to be some kind of extension offset to the left that would have a view of the tennis court. Again it is two storeys. There is ample parking but it was spread around different parts of the estate. It was while I was remembering the photograph; I have a very good pictorial memory, that I heard car engines starting up. It snapped me back to the present. I stayed very still. I could hear the engines rumbling, and then I heard something else that was barely discernible, a footfall on gravel I was sure. I eased up to the first corner keeping low and looked round. I was just in time to see a dark shape walking towards the far bend. He disappeared out of sight. There was enough light now to be able to see vague outlines. I approached the second corner very gingerly. It would be stupid to have to fight at this juncture. I eased round the second corner and the guard was still striding away towards the house, he seemed to be talking into a radio. I remained where I was. I decided to wait in the lane until I heard the convoy move away, half a dozen vehicles were not going to leave silently. However, I feel that the lane in itself is a tunnel that could be a trap so it would be better to wait at the end closest to the house, I set off along it moving quite quickly and as quietly as possible keeping low. If someone approached now that I had attained the house end I had choices. I had spotted a tell tail red light on a surveillance camera positioned in one of the poplars above where I was waiting. It was facing the way I had just walked! No alarms or the sounds of running feet! Or were they too clever for that? I took off my rucksack, opened it and took out the Japanese Noh mask, and put that on. It had been too dark up to present to make out any features and I am determined that I will not be identified. The Noh masked guaranteed my anonymity and, because it is of Japanese origin, may throw any observers an incorrect line of investigation to follow!

I waited for fully ten minutes before I heard the crunch of gravel beneath the wheels of a number of vehicles. They disappeared quite quickly. I waited a further ten minutes. The amount of light had increased as dawn was breaking and so being able to see was becoming less of a problem. Still I waited, everything seemed quiet.

It was around 08:00 before I moved and I did so because I needed to get in to the house, set my incendiary device and leave before it went off. The timer would be set so that when the minute and hour hand reached twelve noon the contact would be made and the coil would begin to heat up. The fire would happen quite quickly after that. Then I would need to be away before all hell broke loose and we had the fire brigade and police around.

I donned my rucksack and headed out of the lane to my left. I was wearing my gloves now and my hand gun was loaded and ready. The hedge on my left headed towards the boundary of the property and in front there were a couple of small outbuildings and then the manicured lawn up to the front door of the house. There was little cover of any description. I kept to the hedge until I attained the boundary fence. I moved along carefully and quietly until I could see the front door. It was ajar so I waited a little longer. There was a gap in the hedge so I eased through and into a field with some developing winter crop growing. I straightened a little and hurried down, hugging the hedge. I passed the house and arrived at the tennis court. The fence here was not as well maintained so I slipped back into the property and stayed hunkered down and watching the house on my right and the extension/annexe on my left. There was some movement but a strong smell of bacon cooking suggested to me that breakfast must be available. I also was thinking that some room cleaning would take place, possibly this morning; I did not want some hapless person stumbling across my bomb!

Well there was no point in waiting any longer. I decided that the best bet would be the annexe. Probably the rooms for the minor officials and the CIA! It may also be easier to enter that building than the main house. I think that the owners would probably be around somewhere. The annexe was just about up to the boundary; there was enough room for me to slip down the side of the cement rendered structure and to look at the other side. I took my time peering round the corner of the building. It looked more like a prison block than a suitable billet for important visitors. There were windows on this side only and just two that looked like they would provide daylight on a staircase. They were casements that had no open section. The windows along the back had a vertical opener and a smaller high level ventilation section. The ventilators were made from half a dozen glass louvres and all seemed to be in various stages of being open.

The room nearest my current position would be the one furthest away from the entrance and either the first or one of the last to be cleaned. I slipped round the corner to the back of the annexe and stayed low under the first window. My luck was in. I could hear a vacuum cleaner whinging away inside the room. Give the cleaner ten minutes and the room would be clean and highly unlikely to be entered again until this evening. I waited. The minutes passed and then the louvred window was opened wide, a duster was flicked out then, after another couple of minutes I heard a door slam. I guess that is my signal.

I took a last look round where I was going to be standing and there was no one about. I hopped up on to the window ledge pushing my fingers between the plates of glass and hanging on to the frame. The individual plates just slide into a 3-sided metal frame. I lifted two of the pieces of glass out and then slipped them into my pack. This allowed me to get my arm in to open the vertical opener. I was inside within a minute.

The room was plain but well appointed. The wardrobe was a single as was the bed; there was a TV on a stand fixed on the wall high in the corner and a vanity unit. Inside the main door was a second room that held a shower unit and toilet. All fittings were quality but basic. The overall colour scheme was bland touched with red! I looked under the bed and there was some space and a suitcase. In the wardrobe there some clothes, a jacket, trousers and a coat. I checked the drawers and cupboards in the room, there was not much paper available but the clothes and bedding would burn well enough. I set to work taking the device out of my rucksack. I got a couple of polo shirts out of the wardrobe and placed them under the bed making a well in the centre, which I filled with sugar. I then placed the clock and heating coil on the sugar and covered the coil with the thinnest part of the shirt. I soaked the shirts with lighter fuel.

I then took out three balloons filled them with the remains of the lighter fluid and fastened them at various points on the ceiling, headboard and TV. They would help to keep the fire going once it was under way. Finally I set the clock at 11:00 and attached the batteries that set it going. I had half an hour to get away before the room went up. I exited the room as I had entered replacing the louvres and slipped away the same way I had arrived. I was back at the car within the half hour. I changed into the ordinary clothes that I kept in the car and got behind the wheel. I decided to wait and see what the reaction was. It is always the same, no matter how well I prepare I am wary of the final outcome and also more than a little curious! So I waited!

After 45 minutes – nothing! I was beginning to get worried then I heard in the distance two-tone sirens. Yes!! I used my sniper sight and looked back to the estate. I could pick up a plume of smoke that was quite well developed. Well as long as there are no casualties I am happy. The third target had been achieved. Finally, I needed to see some reaction. There is no way of keeping a fire brigade call out to this estate a secret. It will depend what story they tell! Maybe they need a little help!

Chapter 4

Local newspapers being as they are would probably not show any details of the fire or of the accident in the shopping centre for another week. The incident with the cars would not have been reported.

I decided to check out of the Fox and head north but buying national dailies and listening to local radio on my way home. I set off at mid-morning reasoning that there is nothing to gain by hanging around. The day is bright and crisp but cool, a typical autumn day. The trees that were seemingly rushing by the car windows are changing to their winter garb making certain stretches of the drab motorway a riot of colour. Sometimes we don't appreciate the qualities of the country we live in and the journey was marginally more interesting also.

My thoughts inevitably turned towards the next steps that I needed to take. Several questions spring to my mind. What could be done if there was no reaction at all? The authorities both at home and in the US may want to keep a lid on the events of the last three days. Even if there was some reaction in the media, what effect, if any, would that have on the UK/US relationship? Finally, how could I raise the level of animosity between the two governments?

One aspect of the situation that could affect me directly would be if the security services started looking for me. At no time have I felt that there would be any pursuit although I had taken so many precautions during my stay. It is somewhat easier in this country in that you do not have to prove your home address by leaving a passport or other ID particularly in a pub where all they want is to make money. I had paid for everything by cash as I tend to everywhere I go. As a matter of course I constantly check my rear view mirror when I am driving and even when out walking I take the opportunity to glance around to try and spot any followers. Also I had not revealed where I am from in conversation with anyone. I am very good at letting other people talk while I listen and nod or grunt in the appropriate places. By following that principle it's amazing how much you learn and how little you give away! People do not like silences and so they will talk to fill a void and they reveal all sorts of interesting information.

I was home by the middle of the afternoon and, it being Saturday, there was no one about. Bill and Stacey do not work weekends unless I have a special request. It gives me some private time. I needed to peruse the newspapers I had bought earlier and then I would get in touch with Sumisu to see if he had any information for me.

There was an article in the Daily Mail reporting that two fire appliances had been sent to a private estate on the outskirts of Westerham. Police are investigating the cause of the fire. I allowed myself a little smile! I could find nothing about a CIA man ending up in hospital, which doesn't really surprise me. I suppose that the initial reaction would be between the two governments and us plebs would only hear final platitudes that governments agreed upon and that they felt would mollify the media.

I sent a message to Sumisu asking for any further news and then was very lazy and drove down to the annexe. I needed to sort out the car and the gear employed down south. I also did a short work out to remove the tension in my neck and shoulders, then showered and strolled back to my flat. By the time I had returned to the apartment I had heard nothing so it would be relaxation and a planned walk on to the pub this evening.

Maintaining my 'normal' life included church on Sunday morning. Most of my pub pals went as well. It was a great way of being part of the community but there was also that continual niggle in the back of my mind about the things I have done and will do in the future. They do not match with a Christian lifestyle. I felt that the only reasonable course of action would be to stop going to church because I cannot see me giving up my work for a long time. There are too many injustices going on that I feel I can 'sort' where the authorities are handcuffed! On the other hand stopping going to church would certainly draw attention to myself, I would have to continue that internal battle and probably end up having some kind of discussion with the parish priest but that bridge would be crossed if and when it arose.

I was just sitting down in the apartment to relax when the intercom summoned me. It was Sumisu and Naomi. I invited them in and when formalities were observed and the green tea served Sumisu apprised me of the reason for his visit.

"Patrick san we have some photographs of the farm and an article from a local paper that may be of interest to you. You did remarkably well as a fire-raiser! The article states that an American was admitted to the local hospital with a suspected broken leg after an accident in the local shopping precinct. He was treated and later released. A very productive few days!" he stated. "However, we have no reports of any friction between the two camps. That does not mean that there hasn't been. In fact there has been no report of any description. The silence is deafening! The conclusion I draw from that is there has been a significant problem and no conclusions have been drawn which probably will result in a subsequent meeting and you can guarantee that it won't be on British soil." He finished.

"So Sumisu san what are your suggestions?" I enquired. "Do we wait until another venue is announced? Do we contact the French and German secret services and apprise them of our feelings about the USA and the threat to their states and economies?"

"The short answer Patrick san is 'Yes' to both of your questions. That is where Naomi san will be of assistance. Her skills as a translator I have already informed you of, but she is also representing our great nation, in an unofficial capacity. What I suggest is that you travel to France and move on with your plans to complete the purchase of that property of yours and take Naomi san with you. There we will set up a meeting with the DCRI - Central Directorate of Interior Intelligence, their spy organisation! At that meeting all you can do is explain your feelings about the way things are in the UK and how they may be in the future for France. You need to also tell the French that UK sovereignty and independence would be better served by closer links with Europe and to that end you will also be talking to the Federal Information Service (BND) of Germany.

That is all that can be done for now. The intelligence agencies of those two countries will begin to look at the situation from their own viewpoint and may or may not contact us in the future." He finished with a sigh.

"The property in France is almost habitable but it may be politic to book a hotel in the town." I said. "The nearest town is La Forge about 5 miles northeast of Le Mans - it has hotels. The house is to the northwest of La Forge. I will book us a couple of rooms but how soon…?" I began.

"As soon as possible Patrick san," he interrupted. "We need to be ready for the next finance meeting with the Americans."

"Ok there is a place that has chambre d'hotes called La Villa des Arts. I will book us in today and we will leave Tuesday. France is closed on Mondays! It will take us around 10 hours to drive there so we will leave here at 02:00 to get the early train under the channel and then we will be in La Forge by late afternoon." I stated. "If you could be here tomorrow evening Naomi san?"

She blushed very prettily and turned her almond eyes full on to me; it made me catch my breath, and replied,

"Of course, Patrick san I will be ready."

She was in control again and quite assertive but I shall never forget that blush and those deep dark brown eyes.

"Thank you for your hospitality Patrick san we will leave now." My mentor stated.

With that they stood and bowed, Naomi gave a small smile and they left.

Perhaps I am not one of the world's greatest thinkers but Sumisu had just made my plans gel into something that will help us to make progress of sorts. I would explain to the Fordyce's that I was going to the new house in France to sign the purchase agreement, I was paying cash so that would go through quickly, even for France. I couldn't therefore give them a return date. I went on to the pub, which is a break in my usual habits but I made the excuse I fancied a change. I let slip that I was going to look at a house in France this week with a view to buying it. I told my pals where it is approximately and the fact that it would be available to them for breaks if I'm not using it!

The following day was busy, but productive and by the time Naomi arrived, alone, everything was prepared. She was dressed smart casual in a pale grey V-necked jumper over navy slacks and looking very relaxed and confident. Perhaps Sumisu made her nervous. We chatted for a little while and then I let her have my bed and I rested on the sofa. We needed to be fresh for the journey. At 01:00 my alarm sounded and I got up, showered and dressed. By the time I had made coffee for us both, she seemed to be more westernised than Sumisu, Naomi was also ready to go.

I had decided that we would travel in the Jaguar XF Portfolio, there was no contest really, it would be very comfortable and it is not tricky to drive so Naomi could share the workload. When travelling similarly with friends we tend to take a short break every couple of hours or so that helps to stave off tiredness, and that was the way it was. Naomi drove very sensibly and quickly when it was her turn and we were in France before 09:00 when we stopped for croissants and coffee.

All the time we had been together we chatted amiably on a superficial level, friendly enough but nothing personal. Over coffee, French quality, I asked her about home and

Gurentai and her involvement. She was not very forthcoming replying with,

"Patrick it is better if we do not know too much about each other, then if we are required to answer questions by an enemy we cannot be easily coerced."

"Of course, you are correct Naomi!" I replied.

We continued on our journey talking about where we were and the things we could see but not about each other. She was warming up though, or it seemed so to me. We checked in at the La Villa des Arts.

"I can see why you have brought the Jaguar Patrick!" Naomi commented as we pulled into the small car park.

"Yes nice isn't it." I retorted. "We will go and look at my new house when we have unpacked."

It was only a short trip from La Forge and we were there in five minutes. I turned left off the road and pulled up in the ample parking space through the modern archway. There are garages on the left and a swimming pool on the right. We left the car and approached the house. It is a modern brick built structure with six bedrooms, four are en suite and there is also a family bathroom upstairs and the lower floor has a slightly Victorian feel in that there is a library, dining room, games room, office and a den as well as a sumptuous lounge. The kitchen has everything a cordon bleu chef would require including a doorway down to a wine cellar. That would cost some money to stock to its capacity!

The situation of the house was very private. The back and side masked from the road by trees on the northern and eastern side but open farmland to the south gives unrestricted views and exposure to the sun. The windows are all equipped with shutters and the floors are mostly marble tiled with rugs, very expensive rugs, scattered in the various rooms. The lounge and library floors were an exception, made from wood but with a huge Turkish patterned hand-made carpet covering the majority of the floors.

Obviously, I would be stamping my own personality on the house when I moved in so at the moment it looked a little bare but I tried to paint a mental picture for Naomi. It was an enjoyable task for me because I had no one to share my ideas with previously, but I was a little disappointed in her reaction in that she received the knowledge without comment. Still keeping her distance!

"It is very luxurious Patrick" she stated simply.

We headed back to the hotel changed and went out for a sumptuous evening meal at a restaurant in the town. I had chosen a small family run establishment because in the past I have always found them to provide the best service and quality even if the range available is rarely extensive and often seasonal. After a stroll around, a cognac and coffee in a local bar we went back to our rooms for a good night's rest. It had been a very long day.

The following morning I carried out part of the reason for us being in France. I went to the local notary and signed the necessary papers for the purchase of the mini chateau I am buying. I returned to the hotel but never got there. Naomi was sat at a table outside a café drinking coffee so I joined her.

"Good morning Naomi!" I smiled.

"Morning Patrick!" She replied with a smile.

"Have you heard anything from Sumisu?" I asked.

"He has arranged a meeting for us with a Francois Picard in Le Mans today at 15:00. We will set off after lunch Patrick," she instructed.

"Of course Naomi." I responded. I was beginning to suspect that I was being led rather than doing the leading!

After a lunch of salad, cheeses and wine followed by a short siesta, we set off the twelve to fifteen miles it was to the town of Le Mans. It is a city located on the Sarthe River. Traditionally the capital of the province of Maine, it is now the capital of the Sarthe department and the seat of the Roman Catholic diocese of Le Mans. It has been host to the famous 24 Hours of Le Mans sports car race since 1923. It is a very posh place as well, a legacy of the racing crowd that frequent the town annually. So the café where we are meeting Francois Picard was very nice. Both Naomi and I had power dressed deliberately as we suspected that we would be in sumptuous surroundings talking to quite an important guy. Naomi was wearing a grey trouser suit with a gold shirt under the jacket, the shoes were black, highly polished and with a medium heel. She may have been taller than me if the heels had been the size of stilettos some girls wear. I was wearing dark navy slacks, black shoes and a white shirt with a pale blue sweater draped over my shoulders in the French style.

We chose a table against the wall of the café and sheltered from the autumn breeze that was blowing and away from other customers so that we would not be overheard. We were twenty minutes early and had ordered coffee, which arrived just as did Monsieur Picard. We ordered a drink for our guest and settled to chat.

"Good afternoon." He said. His accent was strong but he spoke steadily and without emotion so he was easy to understand. "I think for the purposes of this meeting we do not use our names even though we are aware of them."

"We agree!" replied Naomi before I could speak. He continued,

"As I understand it you have a scenario to put to us."

"Yes." I replied. "I will take you through the situation briefly as I see it remembering that certain significant elements within the illustrious Japanese nation agree to some extent with what I am about to tell you."

He nodded encouragement and Naomi sat back and translated in a quiet and subtle manner.

"For a number of years I have been unhappy about US influence in my country. I have never considered, until now, that there may be a purpose to the way that USA products, mores and political views are bombarding our country. The world is aware of the aggressive nature of the USA Foreign Policy as demonstrated in the Middle East. What I believe is that the UK is also a target!"

Picard was sat facing me with his hands resting on his cup and saucer, looking totally expressionless. I went on,

"I believe that the Americans have started to focus their efforts more directly at us. I have no doubt that you are aware of the recent visit of a party of Financial Representatives to the UK. Their purpose is to align fiscal policies between our two countries. There is also an effort by certain MPs to introduce a gun law similar to that of the US into my country. If that is passed through Parliament and the monetary policies also, we will have been virtually absorbed as the 51st State of the Union." I paused.

"It would seem that there is some possible basis in what you are saying," Picard commented.

"This process has been proceeding for a number of years starting in a small way. As I said earlier, by making aspects of their culture attractive to our young people, which in itself would seem harmless enough, they are exceedingly popular. I do not believe that the majority of the kids in the UK are aware of what being the 51st State would mean to them long term. No free National Health Service or public pension schemes. Conscription to the US armed forces to fight whatever damned wars they chose. There are many aspects of our country that would be lost forever." I stopped.

Picard took a sip of his coffee and glanced out at the passers-by and the square we were looking out on. There is some litter, the usual coffee cups, a MacDonald's restaurant, Game stores and music vendors. No different from any other town or city across the western world. I could almost hear his thought processes.

"I understand why you have arrived at the conclusions you have. The question is your projection of the US influence to the point where you are inextricably linked with them. How accurate could that be? If it all!" he retorted somewhat curtly. "And what has it to do with France?"

I started to bristle as I felt that Picard was belittling my position. Naomi nudged me under the table she misses nothing.

"It is obvious to us in Japan that western influence has a detrimental effect on our culture and there are no circumstances we would endure to come under the influence of the US to the extent it has happened in the UK. However, it would seem to have occurred partly due to the common language and the lengths to which Sir Winston Churchill went to involve them in the 2nd World War, but also because of a shared history." She said. "What concerns us is that access to the UK would also give them influence over what were the

Commonwealth nations and that would make them an almost unassailable world power. That would bring them closer to Japan, China and Russia which in turn would give them almost world domination."

Naomi had spoken in a quiet but very focussed way and watching Picard I could tell he was impressed. She went on,

"I understand France may not be under such a direct threat from America but you only have to look around at this beautiful city to see their influence. The purpose of meeting with you today is to also make a request."

Picard raised his eyebrows,

"And that is?" he responded.

She resumed,

"Having discussed this with our friend here it would seem to us that a peaceful way of restoring the balance would be if the UK was even more closely aligned with France and Germany and the rest of the EU. We would like you to do nothing more than investigate the possibilities of closer links."

The Frenchman stirred his almost empty cup thoughtfully.

"What you are saying is riddled with possibilities but without concrete evidence that what you say is the aim of the Yankees."

I must have looked disappointed because he continued more positively,

"However, you are requesting measures that are possible and I am happy to take your information to my superiors. He smiled. "Now my friends it has been a diverting meeting and I find you a charming couple but I must take my leave. I have a feeling that we may well meet again. Au revoir!"

With that he was gone as if we had never met. I looked at Naomi and said,

"That was easier than I thought it would be. He also said that we were a charming couple!" I said with a wink!

"Forget it Patrick!" she asserted. "We weren't really asking for anything major either. When it comes to future negotiations things may not be as easy!"

Of course she was quite correct as usual. We finished our drinks, paid the bill and left. We took our time strolling back to the car keeping an eye on each other's backs and satisfying ourselves that we hadn't been followed. We got to the Jag and set off back to La Forge chatting amiably as before. Naomi really is a most charming person. I could see aspects of Misaki in her. Misaki who had been murdered by the Mafia three years before! Misaki who had been with me physically if nothing else! Perhaps she is right I didn't want anything bad to happen to Naomi.

"Is everything all right Patrick, you seem a little distracted!" she commented.

"Everything is fine Naomi. I was thinking of something that happened years ago. I replied.

"Misaki?" she stated.

"Well I should not be surprised. You must have been fully briefed before we met." I said.

"Of course but I am sorry about Misaki." She replied.

"Ok. I still blame myself and yes we had a relationship of the purely physical kind." I responded.

We chatted in a relaxed manner for the rest of the journey until we got back to La Villa des Arts. I contacted Sumisu and outlined the content of the meeting. He responded that we now must travel to Munich to meet the BND representative Helmut Hahn and meet him on Friday at 15:00 in the Botanischer Garten on Menzinger Strasse 65 at the cafe. That is going to be a journey and a half as it is over a thousand miles between the two cities, but much of it could be done on motorways thank goodness. I thought carefully about the journey and how best we could carry it out with the minimum amount of exhaustion! We need to get as close to Munich as possible tomorrow and have a relatively short journey on Friday morning, no more than 300 miles I was planning. I used my Samsung Galaxy Tab ipad to check the route and decided that we needed to get as far as Baden-Baden or Karlsruhe by tomorrow evening.

    I went over my plans with Naomi over a final cup of coffee of the day.

"You certainly think of everything Patrick," she commented. "I think it is a good plan. Are you always this thorough?"

"I have to be, it's a weakness! I said in reply. "I have also booked us a suite with separate rooms in the Der Blaue Reiter Hotel on the east side of the city," I went on, "Anyway time for bed. We need to set off at 08:00 at the latest."

    Naomi had a slightly puzzled expression on her face as she said goodnight and kissed me on the cheek. I suppose after three days she was beginning to get to know me and hadn't figured the obsessive-compulsive side of my nature. I went to bed.

We were well on the road by 09:00. The Jaguar was eating up the miles and the autumn weather was being kind. The early morning mist had just about lifted and there looked like a bright day ahead of us. We travelled in a companionable silence with just the odd comment. I kept an eye on the rear view mirror but all was quiet or it seemed so. I wouldn't put it passed Picard to have someone keep an eye on us. We did very well, just changing driver the once and by lunchtime we were in Saarbrucken. The remainder of the journey was just as uneventful.

We arrived at the hotel before six and checked in. I could tell Naomi was impressed. It was beautifully appointed, as a five star hotel should be, but there was one aspect I found garish and vulgar and that was the huge modern art pieces inset behind the bed and in various parts of the public rooms and corridors. No subtlety, and impossible to get away from. However, the quality of the furnishings made up for it. A pity we only had one night here, I would have to put it down as one of my places to revisit on the way to somewhere in the future!

The following day, as for Picard, we dressed formally for Herr Hahn. We were at the botanical gardens early but not nearly early enough to beat Hahn. As we walked in to the tearooms a tall man stood and beckoned to us. I looked round as if surprised anyone would know we were there. He waved again. I conducted Naomi across to where Helmut Hahn was waiting. He knows who we are and why we are here. He wasn't my idea of a German spy. Rather geekish. Tall yes but wearing spectacles and his suit wasn't as immaculate as I would have thought. His smile was genuine enough and he is obviously taken with Naomi from the way that his greeting to me was perfunctory, but almost effusive for Miss Kobayashi!

We chatted about the journey and eventually got round to the reason why we were in his country.

"There is no way the USA will be allowed to have a political influence in our country!" he stated quite forcefully. "We are not as decadent as they and we have a stronger culture."

"I appreciate the strength of your country Herr Hahn but all you need to do is look at the high streets in your cities and you must admit that there is influence there already." I replied.

"So what is it that you need from Germany Mr Steele?" he demanded.

I was expecting Naomi to cut in as she had with Picard but she sat very quietly.

"We would like to strengthen our ties within Europe, even more so than the European Community. To maintain our own sovereignty we need to loosen ties with the USA but would still be vulnerable if alone and so we are speaking to you and have also spoken to similar representatives in France." I said.

"Ah yes Monsieur Picard!" he interrupted.

"At the moment it is a matter of raising your government's awareness of the possible future problems for Europe if we become one of the United States of America!" I concluded.

"And why has Japan become involved?" he asked looking directly at Naomi.

"We are concerned for the long term future of our country and to a degree the rest of the world!" she replied. "If the Yanks have so much influence over the English speaking world….!" She let her statement hang.

"The mere fact that I have been forced into meeting you two today will result in the setting up of an investigation. The length and thoroughness will depend on our initial findings. If you have further evidence please do not hesitate to forward copies to myself as I am sure you will with Picard." He concluded.

With that he stood, shook hands and left. We sat down and I looked at Naomi. She seemed strangely cowed but for no reason that I could discern.

"Is everything ok Naomi?" I asked gently.

"Everything is fine Patrick. I found Herr Hahn aggressive and very off putting. He also showed little respect towards me by ogling which I did not like at all." She responded.

She looked at me full face on, unlike the side long efforts she had fired at Hahn,

"You are very respectful Patrick and I find you easy to talk to, maybe too easy! It has made this job more enjoyable. Thank you." She finished.

I felt quite nervous; embarrassed that she had been so open with me. She is such an attractive girl and I know we must not get involved.

"Thanks for that Naomi," I said staring at her, then my shoes then everywhere else. "We need to find somewhere to stay!"

She laughed, a soft peeling laughter that touched her eyes,

"You English are so hopeless at expressing feelings, even little ones!"

I smiled at her and took her arm as we left the tearooms.

We decided to travel out of Munich and find a small spot on the way back north. We needed to contact Sumisu and let him know what had happened and head back to England. The hotel we found had plenty of vacancies again fortunately because we are out of the holiday season. We booked a couple of rooms and had a very pleasant dinner. Having spoken to

Sumisu we only had to get back home as soon as possible. It would probably be Sunday because we had quite a trip to the channel and a further 250 miles up to Yorkshire. We would break the trip at Calais and be home for early afternoon Sunday. There was no further reference to our previous conversation but we seemed closer somehow but in a friendship sort of way. In fact I know very little about this girl and I don't know how much she knows about me! We have been thrown together rather by our Gurentai association. I assume she is as skilled as I in the art of getting rid of opponents and obviously very bright – a really scary combination!

Chapter 5

The journey home was long but uneventful and Naomi and I chatted like brother and sister. I felt myself on the horns of a dilemma because I found myself attracted to this girl but knowing at the same time it would be dangerous for us to become involved. In some strange way I felt that she is as aware as I, but she is still maintaining a very friendly aura towards me, and this I find extremely pleasant.

We arrived back at my annexe as expected in the middle afternoon. At our previous two-hour stop I'd sent a text message to Sumisu giving our estimated time of arrival, so he was waiting for us. I parked the car up and we strolled up to the apartment discussing our trip.

He seemed satisfied with the outcome and said,

"We will keep the French and Germans up to speed on developments over here. I also have news of the next finance meeting Patrick san. It will take place in Boston in a week's time. I would suggest that you make preparations to be in that city before they arrive."

"I know the area quite well having holidayed in Salem a few years ago. I will leave on Wednesday. When exactly do they arrive?" I asked.

"They're expected in a week or so, on the Monday probably. Their first meeting is the following day. What will you do Patrick san?" he reported.

"Having given this some thought I will carry out similar actions against the Americans as in this country." I stated.

"You will not take action against the UK representatives?" asked Sumisu quizzically.

I was wondering where he was coming from! My thinking is that attacking our own people and their artefacts would suggest only that the US citizens were against the moves but thinking about it, if attacks occurred against the US delegates then it would turn their own people against the UK. That may be a more powerful motivator.

"No – I believe that attacking the US people on their own soil would have a more powerful reaction from the citizenship." I explained.

Sumisu nodded sagely,

"I agree Patrick san!"

That is the first time in our three-year association that my mentor had agreed to one of my plans without equivocation. It made me feel nervous!

They were standing up to leave and I stood also. Sumisu turned to me and said,

"Naomi will meet you there Patrick san. It is better that you travel separately. She will provide backup and any other assistance you require. I suggest you also stay in separate hotels and meet only when necessary as your activities are likely to create keen interest from the FBI and the CIA. Enjoy your trip!" he said.

Naomi gave me a warm smile and a polite bow, which I reciprocated and they left.

The following morning I contacted the travel agent I always use and gave them my requirements. I had woken with the idea that I needed to cover my arrival in the Boston area as much as possible. The security agencies would be screening direct flights into the States for a week before the meetings at least, so I decided a tour, or at least what looks like a tour is the order of the day. I wanted to fly to New York, take an internal flight to Buffalo, ostensibly to visit Niagara Falls where I would pick up a hire car and drive to a hotel in Salem arriving in the eastern city on Friday. The agent seemed ok with my arrangements and organised my outbound flight from Manchester the following day.

I messaged Sumisu and Naomi to let them know the name of the Hotel and my date of arrival.

I decided that I should work out and so ran down to the annexe. Vince Thompson arrived about the same time and we carried out a gentle exercise programme and some meditation then I did some weight training. Stacey and Bill arrived together which I thought was odd. Stacey usually drops Bill and then goes up to the apartment. I went into the kitchen to make a drink and they followed me.

"Good Morning." I said cheerily, "What can I do for you two?"

They were looking like two school kids in front of the head teacher because they had done something wrong.

"Well," Bill started, "We were wondering what your intentions are concerning the apartment and this place, what with you buying a property in France and all!"

I paused. From their point of view they had concerns for their livelihood. I am away so much they must have been concerned that I was going to emigrate or something.

"I see," I smiled my most reassuring smile, "Bill, Stacey you have nothing to worry about. I know I am away much of the time and indeed I am off to the USA tomorrow, but this town is my home and I will never want to live permanently anywhere else. If you are happy working for me you have a job for life. Do you want shorter hours or different working conditions?" I asked.

"No no!" said Stacey hurriedly, "Bill – I said we shouldn't say anything!"

"It's all right Stacey!" I interrupted.

"We are very happy working for you Patrick. In fact it's a bit of a cushy number really. We would be mortified to lose this position. It is just with yon Jap bloke and you being off, well we weren't sure." Bill explained.

Quite a speech from the guy he is a man of very few words usually, outwardly a dour Yorkshire man.

"Well the Japanese gentleman is one of my bosses in fact. He represents a large firm that has worldwide clients and he is linking me with some of these high value clients to manage their accounts. I am really just the public face of the accountancy firm. I also work for other people as well, although with all the travelling, not so much as I used to. Really I can turn down or accept work but at my age I am doing as much as I can at present. Eventually I will slow down and spend more time at home." I explained.

"Thanks for that Patrick," Stacey said. "There is just one other thing."

"Yes!" I said

"I have a nephew Patrick who is a proper handful. He's giving my sister lots of headaches. He dropped out of school, has had bits and pieces of jobs and is hanging about with a right horrible bunch. Do you know anyone who might have a position for him?" asked Stacey.

"Look Stacey I am away from tomorrow for almost a fortnight. I will have a think and see what I can come up with. Is that ok?" I said.

"Thanks Patrick." She said and set off up to the flat without another word.

"Bill I could do with a lift to Manchester airport leaving here at 04:00. Is that ok?" I requested.

"Fine Patrick I'll be here. Listen Patrick about our Ethan. You don't have to do anything if it's difficult." He mumbled.

"Ethan, your nephew?" he nodded, "Why don't you bring him down here to meet Vince while I'm away, use the gym and the weights and such. Obviously he would be your responsibility but it might keep him out of mischief for a couple of weeks. Give him some small jobs to do. Paint the outside of the living quarters, log his hours and tell him I'll pay him when I get back. I'll start him on minimum wage." I said.

"Thanks Patrick that will be a great help and Stacey will be well made up," he replied.

"See you in the early hours then Bill!" and with that I left.

As I walked up to the flat I pondered what I had done for the Fordyce's. Was I turning into a saint!

The flight itself was comfortable as it should be in business class. I arrived at Newark New Jersey at 18:00. I caught a yellow cab to my fairly standard hotel. The atmosphere in New York you could cut with a knife it was so humid. The air con in the cab wasn't working! By the time I got to the hotel in the gathering dusk I was soaked. The cabby knew two things, how to talk and how to drive but not how to shut up! The longest half an hour of my life so far!! The hotel was comfortable without being flashy, but as is the fashion, no restaurant. I am only staying two nights so unpacking was not necessary. All I took out of my case were the ceramic weapons I had brought! They would stay with me.

I found another cab, this time with working air conditioning and went to Chinatown for supper.

The following day was spent taking in some of the sights, Empire State, Time Square and the Statue of Liberty, a real tourist trip and even had time for a show on Broadway!

Thursday morning I was up and off back to the airport for an internal flight to Buffalo. The flight was less than an hour but rough nevertheless. The pilot was either training or semi-retired and a bit rusty and the trolley dollies were rather well used. If you want to know where old airhostesses go to, try Continental Airlines internal flights! When I arrived at the airport and disembarked I went to the car hire desk to pick up the vehicle that had been booked for me. The next part of my trip was a lengthy drive to the East coast and Salem staying overnight Friday and Saturday.

The Niagara Falls is breath taking and I spent some time watching the sheer power as the water tumbled down into the steaming cauldron beneath where the Maid of the Mist plied its trade. It's rather disturbing to think that the Falls is managed to about two thirds capacity. The hotel I am staying in is the Days Inn on the River, a 4 star pile with luxury restaurant that is going to serve me a sumptuous steak meal. American restaurants struggle with quality and range of cooking but they do excellent steaks and try to make up for their culinary failings with quantity!

Friday morning I set off eastwards and drove hard all day. I found a hotel in a provincial town that had been bypassed by the highway and was dying quietly by the old railroad. It had been a major stop off point close to an important rail junction. I think I was the only person staying there and the facilities were from the last century! The foyer was full of photographs of presidents that had stayed in the hotel in years gone by.

Saturday I breakfasted in a traditional diner before setting off again. After another overnight in a Premier Inn style hotel I continued on my way to Salem. It is close enough to Boston for ease of access and far enough away that my arrival will create no stir! The hotel is the five stars Amelia Payson House and is beautifully appointed. I checked in and was shown to a large suite with two bedrooms a lounge and a bathroom! A little over the top but as the season is quiet in November and the hotel quite empty my money bought me a good deal more than it would at the height of the season! The staff is very friendly and I felt welcome. As usual this is only a bed and breakfast hotel so I set off into the town to find a suitable place to eat. The choice was limited to steak, Chinese or Italian food. I went to the yacht club on the recommendation of a taxi driver and ate fish, which was passable, before returning to my room in the Amelia Payson.

I was just settling down to sleep when there was the tell-tale vibration of my mobile. A message from Sumisu! Simple and to the point he had sent *"Meet in Boston for lunch tomorrow – time and place later"*

The following morning I drove, or tried to drive into Boston for 10:00. It was a worse experience than driving on the M25 in the rush hour! Just arterial car parking! As I was sat biding my time on the main highway I received another text that simply said '*The Boston Coffee Co. on Salem Street. 11:00'* I programmed that into the GPS and five minutes later continued the crawl towards my destination. I just about got there at the allotted time; needless to say Sumisu was waiting for me. He was alone, no sign of Naomi. I felt ever so slightly disappointed.

"Good morning Patrick san." He said cheerily.

I was slightly less so and gave out a somewhat disgruntled,

"Hello Sumisu san!"

"You seem a little out of sorts Patrick san. It may be useful to consider that having time to contemplate and reflect on the future as well as the past is a gift!" he countered.

I was dumbstruck. I'd been admonished again for failing to make the best use of my time.

"Of course you are right Sumisu san." I replied.

The place was heaving with bodies, even though we were in autumn it was still quite warm and the odour of coffee was powerful. Even so the atmosphere was friendly and too busy for us to be easily overheard. I suppose that is why he chose this place.

"They will arrive today Patrick san. They are staying in the five star Hotel Veritas in the Cambridge district a short walk from the Harvard University. I believe that the intention is to hold the meetings in the University. It makes sense with the students in session the place will be busy and it will be difficult to get at them! A wise choice!" commented Sumisu.

I sipped my coffee and considered what might be done.

"The USA delegates are staying at The Charles Hotel which is a little further away on the opposite side of the University to the Veritas. Certainly not putting all their eggs in one basket! However, that hotel is a little more isolated on the edge of John F Kennedy Park, and may offer the opportunities you require!" stated Sumisu.

"Sumisu san I thought you said that Naomi would be joining us?" I said changing the subject.

"She is here already Patrick san and is in fact staying in Boston as a student of Spanish at Harvard. She has a room in the university as an overseas student. Convenient don't you think Patrick san." He said. "I am informed that she has located the meeting rooms and some of the timings of those meetings, which may be helpful because it will give us some indication of when the two delegations will move." He explained.

"Yes Sumisu san!" I responded, but my mind was blank. There are so many other things I need to know, for instance, who are the members of the delegation from the US Government?

At that moment Naomi came and joined us looking very much the student in denims, tucked in shirt and jumper tied round her shoulders.

"Good morning Sumisu san, Patrick san." No bow, perhaps she was getting right into character! "I trust you are both well?" she asked.

We responded favourably and chatted amiably enough for a few minutes re-establishing our acquaintanceship. She seemed to be enjoying her course although at 28 she was a good bit above the average age of the rest of her colleagues.

"There are meetings every day from 08:00 until lunchtime and then again from 14:00 until 18:00. The plan is that the meetings will be over by Friday and the UK representatives will return home at the weekend." Naomi explained. "The US team have arrived and they are surrounded with their usual bodyguards and the FBI also, this is not going to be easy Patrick. Please be careful!" she stated.

"I did right driving here, it is the only way to enter the city unchecked, but they will keep an eye on the hotels so I will stay in Salem." I said. "The actions are going to be somewhat trickier so I will spend the rest of the day in the park, and near The Charles just to see what I can find out. Maybe take a meal at Tommy Doyle's in Harvard Square before going back to Salem. Would you two like to meet me there say 19:00? I can share what I find out." I concluded.

"It may be better if we do not meet as a threesome again Patrick san. Meet with Naomi tonight and let her know of any equipment you may need I will meet each of you separately tomorrow if necessary." suggested my mentor.

With that, and after a few more minutes of pleasantries, I left and headed for Cambridge in the hire car.

The area around The Charles was a mixture of University buildings, period shops and student accommodation, and everywhere were small numbers of parking spaces. I found one opposite The Charles on the same side of the square as the hotel. I left the car and strolled towards the JFK Park in the afternoon's watery sunlight. I wandered over the beautifully manicured grass beneath the trees that are changing to the wonderful God painted shades of browns, reds and yellows. Walking along the park footpath parallel with the back of the hotel I spotted a restaurant very close to the back of The Charles, called Legal Sea Foods. That could be very handy!

I continued up the side of the hotel and was aware that an ordinary looking man wearing a blazer and sporting an earpiece is watching me from a side door. I didn't indicate that I had noticed and just kept walking towards the square about 100 yards in front of me. At the main entrance of the hotel there is yet another guy stood around doing nothing other than watching everyone who passes by or enters the hotel. I kept going turning left and continuing my visual research. I angled away from the hotel because I am sure these guys will talk to each other relaying who is passing.

I completed the final half at a much greater distance and with my jacket over my arm subtly changing my appearance. My conclusions were succinct - it was going to be impossible to get in and out of the hotel easily!

Now it was a matter of looking at what possibilities there were, that would cause consternation as well as disruption. One idea that immediately sprung to mind is tampering with their food particularly if any of them are keen on seafood. Maybe another attack on their vehicles and finally perhaps a bomb scare in the university!! Simple but very annoying! That will do for starters and they require a minimum amount of preparation and equipment. I feel more positive already!

I spent the rest of the day taking in the sights of Boston and doing some shopping! By 18:45 I had arrived at Tommy Doyle's and was waiting for the arrival of Naomi Kobayashi. I couldn't help but feel a little bubble of excitement at the idea of having some private time with this Japanese doll! I admonished myself silently. There is no chance that we can have a satisfactory relationship partly because of the death of Misaki and partly because there was no way we could both continue in this work and be together.

She announced her presence with a hand on my shoulder and a kiss on the cheek, and a cheery,

"Hi!"

"Hello!" I replied just as pleasantly but feeling slightly puzzled after my most recent thoughts. She obviously picked up on my puzzlement because she continued almost whispering,

"I am a student Patrick!"

"Of course, Naomi. Forgive me I am being thick!" I commented.

For which I received a none too gentle kick on the shins, at which we both laughed. We ordered food, and spent a very pleasant couple of hours chatting, eating and drinking. At coffee time I outlined what I was hoping to do and asked for certain equipment. It was a relatively short list and hopefully easily accessible materials. I requested a fast acting emetic or laxative and a small toolkit that could be used for disconnecting brake lines or otherwise tampering with the functionality of the vehicles. Explosives were out of the question because there would be sniffer dogs and sniping in this terrain would be impossible so it would be mechanical failure they would experience.

Naomi told me that she didn't require a ride and so left the same way she arrived kissing me and patting my shoulder! I paid the bill using cash and set off back to Salem, the home of the Witch Trials of 1692 when around 26 people were imprisoned and died, in the dark! The journey was trouble free! I was back at the Amelia Payson a lot faster than I crawled to Boston! After a coffee and a brandy, I couldn't get a decent whisky, I went to bed. My plans for the next day were to be at the Americans hotel before they got up in the morning. Time is short and I need to move fast so the more information I can collect the better. I set my alarm for 04:30

and using some relaxation techniques learned from Vince - I fell straight asleep.

By 05:30 I was in Boston, in the dark, although dawn was beginning to break, and had found the entrance to the underground garage. I was wearing a black hoodie, black denims and trainers and I kept the hood up and my head down. This modern age of surveillance was no less being followed in Boston as everywhere else in the world. There are cameras on every street corner and plenty round the hotel. I walked purposefully but tried to mask my presence by sticking to the tree lined walkways trying not to make it too obvious. My passage had to appear normal. I found the garage to be protected by a steel door that would scroll up and down as necessary, no access that way but there would be access from inside the hotel. The hotel is open to the public so anyone can walk in and then it would be a case of staying in and accessing vehicles, and maybe food. Then all I have to do is get away!

I went round the hotel and so no obvious signs of guards but I had no doubt they would be there. I circled back to John F Kennedy Park and approached the seafood restaurant directly from the rear. This smaller building acted well as a barrier between the hotel and my position. I wanted to see the layout as it maybe that this was the place where I could use the chemicals on one or more of the US party. I had a basic idea about the disruption at Harvard and it could be a job for Naomi! I returned to the car and took off my hoodie and replaced it with an open-necked shirt and my trainers for black leather shoes. Picked up a more formal jacket and donned that then strolled into Harvard Square to find a diner where I could eat breakfast, looking like a guy on his way to the office. I finally settled on Charlie's Kitchen where I ordered the Yankee equivalent of full English, minus the hash browns. I was persuaded to have pancakes and maple syrup as well. There were a few people already eating and I was astounded at what I observed. There was one man who must have weighed 20 stone having a similar meal to myself but he was eating bacon and then pancakes then egg and pancakes then hash brown and pancakes! I ate the savoury and started a pancake but was defeated. It seemed to swell in my mouth like a giant whelk!

I had chosen a window seat that looked out at the hotel. I was on my second refill of coffee when at 07:30 a convoy of vehicles emerged from the side street where the hotel garage entrance was situated. I took out my phone and snapped as many of the vehicles as I could unable to be sure of the quality through the plate glass window of the shop. I may need to attack the vehicles away from the hotel so identifying them is essential. I paid my bill and left.

Next job is to go to the university and try and find aforementioned vehicles. I sent a message to Naomi to tell her that I was coming to the university.

No reply, she must be busy.

I was there within twenty minutes and after scouting around I found a parking spot and strolled to a coffee bar frequented by the students. I had so much caffeine this morning I could feel every nerve tingling! I saw nothing unusual but fell lucky when I heard a couple of kids discussing the convoy that had arrived a few minutes earlier.

Apparently, the rumour mill was working at full tilt; they were important government people meeting in the politics department! Well I never! So tomorrow I would have to swing into action.

Chapter 6

My plan is to get into The Charles Hotel this afternoon or early evening and start the disruption immediately. I only have three more days to work my magic! I sent a text message to Sumisu and copied in Naomi. The gist of which is '*let me have my equipment soonest*!' While waiting for a reply I strolled round the campus picking out landmarks and signposts. I'm fortunate that I have the sort of memory for directions that other folk envy. After visiting a place only once I can find my way back very easily. I am using the time so that in the event of having to make a sudden retreat I at least know where I'm heading.

'*Naomi, campus refectory 11:30*' was the message that came in a few minutes later. As it was 10:45 I decided to complete the reconnoitre first and then make my way to the refectory. Once inside the walls of this particular 'grove of academe' and while on my way, I endeavoured to take one or two wrong turnings! It enabled me to find the cameras, fire alarm boxes and sprinklers! The latter occurred in all the corridors about every ten feet; the alarms on all main corridors, and similarly the cameras.

I was already seated and having yet another coffee when I felt the now customary greeting. It just made me smile!

"Why are you grinning like the Cheshire Cat Patrick?" Naomi asked.

"Good morning Naomi. No reason!" I lied with a grin. I just really enjoyed the greeting and the attention it drew from onlookers!

I felt something touch my knee under the table. I took a wrapped parcel around 30 cm long and half as wide and slipped the parcel under my jacket, which was folded, over my knee.

"Thank you Naomi. There is one more thing I would ask of you." I said.

"Yes.....!" she replied quizzically.

"Don't look like that. It's simple and of little or no risk to yourself. All I would like you to do is set off the sprinklers during one of their meetings, and once they are working hit the fire alarms and leave! The only problem you will have is the cameras on every corner of almost all of the corridors but I'm sure you will cope with those." I explained.

She looked at me as if I was stupid,

"Patrick, I have had very similar training to you. We should have an Aikido training session together when we arrive back in England! Yes I can carry out your wishes. This is going to upset the Americans and they will begin to peruse the records of all those people who have recently arrived in Boston and how they came to be here. The agencies will check students, and particularly foreign students. They will find me straight away. I must vanish as soon as you carry out your first action," she stated.

I thought about my original ideas and what Naomi had just told me and what she was saying made perfect sense. In fact I wondered why they hadn't got on to her by now, but she is such a recent arrival that she may have sneaked in after the majority of the screening had been done. On the other hand it could be quite useful to give the delegates a soaking to begin with and then follow it up with another couple of inconveniences. I also realised that we needed to publicise the misfortunes of our party while in the states. There would be no guarantee that the Yanks would share their misfortune with the media.

"Maybe you should carry out your part today! It takes no equipment and while I am here I can take photos of the dripping delegates!" I suggested. "Afterwards you can come back to Salem with me and stay there. No strings!" I added.

She smiled knowingly and said,

"That sounds like a good idea Patrick!"

"Ok then, give me twenty minutes to get to a position outside of the centre they are using for the talks and then on you go." I instructed, "I'm parked close by but I suggest that you make your way to Tommy Doyle's bar and I'll pick you up there."

She agreed and also suggested that she would have to get as close to the Politics Centre as she can because the alarm systems may well be on different circuits. This university is made up of a large collection of buildings and annexes so she is almost definitely right. Why didn't I think of that?

She took her leave and I arranged to meet her at Tommy Doyle's at 15:00.

I watched her retreating form and was as impressed as every other red blooded male in the café who caught that picture! The scary thing about her is that they don't know how dangerous she can be!

I left a couple of minutes later and headed for the target annexe. The University is quite green, so there are numbers of opportunities to sit on the soft grass and soak up the sun or lean against the bole of a sturdy tree and eat lunch. The weather was ok so I didn't look like 'jimmy no mates' sat against a convenient tree taking an imaginary call on my mobile. I had another five minutes to wait before Naomi Kobayashi went into action. The doorways were flanked by a couple of guys that looked too old for university and built like two members of the Boston Red Sox. Like they are not obvious! On top of those guys I noticed another 'unlikely' strolling aimlessly backwards and forwards along the path in front of the building. There were cameras on the corners of the buildings and I had no doubt that I would be there on the records. The trick is to angle the head downwards and not look at the cameras, as well as doing nothing to draw attention to oneself. I continued pretending to talk into the telephone and when I had 'finished' I turned on the camera and positioned it on my book facing the entrance door of the building.

I didn't have long to wait until the sound of a fire alarm went off. People round about stopped and turned towards the sound then walked on more slowly or watched more intently depending on their nature.

Very soon people started to leave the building holding books and various items of clothing over their heads and looking slightly damp. I started snapping away and there were our VIPs being trooped out by the equally moist bodyguards who then took them straight away clutching their guns under their arms. I had what was required and joined the crowd of people walking away from the building, in the same direction as the wet delegates but being careful not to get too close. It was like observing a group of schoolchildren, albeit slightly elderly in some cases, being shepherded to their next class. They turned right and were taken into another red brick building and I kept going.

    At 15:00 I was waiting for Naomi in Tommy Doyle's, she arrived shortly after me, and after a quick drink we set off back to Salem. This time I was particularly careful about being followed and I set Naomi the task of keeping close watch on drivers following unusual patterns of behaviour. They could be using such techniques as overtaking then dropping back and changing with a different vehicle. We arrived in Salem incident free and went to my hotel. I felt that if we could ensure no one was aware that Naomi was with me then it would make life easier for her - certainly. There was no one in the foyer so we went straight up to my suite and I showed Naomi the facilities. There was a spare room so she would be guaranteed her privacy, if that was what she wanted!

    Once we were settled in I showed Naomi the photographs I had taken. We isolated the snaps of the UK and US delegates and then printed out the snapshots that we wanted to look at more thoroughly. After an agreeable discussion we decided to send the photographs to my local newspaper as well as the national dailies. I also texted the photographs to Sumisu and awaited his response.

"Well done Naomi I believe that was a fairly successful enterprise." I commented. "What are you going to do next?"

"Watch your back Patrick, as usual!" she said.

I obviously looked surprised she went on,

"Sumisu san has us working in threes like this. He probably runs other teams as well but there are only the three of us and I am unaware of the existence of other teams," she commented, "Then he has one person leading, that's you Patrick, and then someone like me to carry out support tasks and to provide additional protection for the actor in the group!"

"I thought that was the way it worked Naomi," I replied, "so tomorrow evening I will be getting into the hotel and either tampering with their food or perhaps their vehicles. If time allows I would like to deal with both. Now I've spotted a seafood restaurant at the back of the hotel, and I think maybe one or two of these guys may like that type of food, so it was my intention of lacing their food with the emetic you have supplied at that place. I just need to know if any of them eat at the seafood restaurant."

"If I might make a different suggestion Patrick, if you keep the two events separate and finish with the vehicles," she said.

It made perfect sense of course!

"How long have you worked with Sumisu san Naomi?" I asked.

"A couple of years, so I have had that pleasure for about the same length of time as you Patrick," she replied in a rather challenging tone.

"Ok! Ok! I was just asking how long, not asking how much more experienced you are!" I replied.

"Sorry Patrick. As a woman working with men I am not always taken seriously!" She said rather more sheepishly.

"We have to trust each other and I was only trying to find out a little more about you. We cannot get into personal details so I thought if we could build some trust on a professional level that it might help!" I said.

"Of course, Patrick you are right." This was more positive. "I have taken part in four other activities one as leader and the rest as support. I am enjoying working with you Patrick, perhaps more than I should," she blushed as she said this.

We sat quietly in my room contemplating what she had just revealed. I've gone over this situation umpteen times in my head, I know we shouldn't get close to each other but the way these mini units work we are all thrust together intensely albeit for a relatively short period of time. The level of trust is as high as it could possibly be, so some connection between the operatives is inevitable. This girl is physically very fit and confident and being Asian I find her attractive, but that's just me! I didn't want to get too close because of what happened to Misaki but I am drawn to Naomi.

"Patrick I understand how you feel about relationships with colleagues after what happened to Misaki," (was she reading my mind?) "I also appreciate from a professional point of view a relationship could seriously influence how we perform in the field, but I would like you to know that I am drawn to you also!" she said as a statement of fact.

There it was out in the open. We both felt similarly and were just as confused about where we go from here but the fact is we are working together at the moment and that is how it is.

"Naomi I understand how you feel and I think that if we were in a situation where we were free to follow our own wishes then it would be different, but at the moment all we can do is be there for each other in the situation in which we find ourselves." I said.

I immediately realised how crap that must have sounded! I leant over and kissed her.

She was surprised and I believe pleased judging from the way she responded.

"I think we need to set off early tomorrow and try to get into the Charles Hotel unnoticed. It may happen that early in the morning the guards could be in a careless frame of mind and that may allow us some access to the garage!" I stated. "Let's find a place to eat and turn in early!"

Naomi smiled and donned a jacket and we left to find a suitable restaurant. It was a pleasant evening strolling round

Salem, which is a delightfully historical town in spite of its gory reputation. We found a place to eat down on the quayside that served fish mostly and just enjoyed each other's company. I'd managed to sneak Naomi in and out of the hotel and there was no problem getting back either. The proprietors of the hotel were very relaxed and accommodating and so I was allowed to get my own key from behind the reception. We got back to the suite and retired to our own segment of the suite. There was little conversation before we turned in. I think Naomi was nervous! We set alarms for 05:00 and settled down for the night.

The following morning we were in Boston before 06:00 armed and ready for action. I had my ceramic handgun and knife. I know Naomi is armed but unaware of her preferences. We parked in a spare space in the sparsely populated car park of a block of flats close to The Charles. We were dressed in city clothes and made for the front door of the Hotel. We followed the signs for the restaurant and went in and had breakfast. I'd brought the toolkit and emetic powder that had been supplied to me by the Gurentai. I was prepared for both scenarios. We took our time and enjoyed each other's company for a little while longer. As time passed the restaurant became busier and would you believe it our delegates came down to eat! It all seemed very normal! They ate in groups and the agents with them ate in turn also but sat at different tables close by. I took the emetic out of my pack. It was in powder form in a small dark brown bottle. The question is how to get to some of the evil stuff on to their food?

We sat and watched for a few minutes and noticed that there was one guy who put small portions on his plate but made repeated trips to the buffet.

The next time he got up to go back to the food serving area I would follow him closely. It didn't take long and in fact he followed a colleague who had just arrived in the dining room. They chatted amiably and I attached myself to the queue immediately behind them. I had a plate in my left hand and put some fried bacon and scrambled egg on it, with my right I was unscrewing the bottle and removing it from my pocket. While they were chatting I edged as closely as I could and sprinkled some of the powder, which resembled pepper, on to the delegate's plate. I was also able to do the same to the guard's food. I finished loading my plate and returned to our table. Naomi and I stayed chatting and eating for a few minutes and then we heard a strangulated gurgling sound and the American delegate left the dining room rapidly followed swiftly by the guard that I had also targeted with his hand over his mouth.

    Naomi and I looked at each other and, unhurriedly finished our meal, rose and left the dining room. I turned right and walked deeper into the bowels of the hotel, whereas Naomi turned left and went out of the revolving doors into the street. I headed for the Gents washroom, taking note of the signs that peppered the walls. Apart from room numbers there were a plethora of fire exit signs, I continued into the washroom making sure I wasn't being followed. This was obviously not the one being used by my victims! There was no one about, so I took a second or two to compose myself and gently left the facilities, pausing outside the door to check the corridor. Instead of going back towards reception I headed further into the corridors on the ground floor until I arrived at a lift, elevator in the US! I hit the basement button and as soon as the doors began to open I stepped through and slid to my right with my hand on my handgun in the small of my back. I kept very still, listening to the sounds of the rather bare and functional corridor in which I found myself. There were no signs on the walls down here; I think I had found some kind of service lift. There were baskets of washing and I could feel the dampness in the air. Somewhere nearby is the laundry. Most of the action down here would be after guests have left for the day.

    I continued my search passing the source of the humidity, the laundry, and eventually coming to a carpeted corridor crossing my path at the other side of a set of double doors. The signs were back again and the garage was on my left. I was still lucky in not having seen a soul. I slipped through the heavy door that separated the garage from the rest of the hotel and found myself in a short concrete lined tunnel with a door at the end opening inwards allowing access to the pillared, echoing cavern that was the car storage facility. I slipped away from the door and stayed quiet in a shadowy alcove for a full five minutes. It is strange but even in a place where there are no other people there is never absolute silence. I could hear dripping, rustlings and scrapings but never identified the sources. What I didn't hear were the sounds of human beings. I didn't altogether trust my own senses but still I could detect no one else in the place.

    The atmosphere was musty and slightly damp and although I could detect nothing audible I noticed an instantly recognisable odour. Someone was or had been smoking. I kept very still for a minute or more and then I heard it - the indisputable sound of a shoe scraping against the concrete floor. I rose up on to the balls of my feet and ever so slowly moved further away from the door. I took the ceramic gun from my waistband and held it two handed in front of me but pointed downwards. I felt sure that whoever it was must have heard me enter the garage so why wasn't he/she making efforts to find me?

I was moving along the wall and trying to watch my direction of travel as well as looking out for what I was thinking is a guard. After another couple of minutes I heard a hushed voice and realised I was in trouble. He was talking on a mobile phone! I can easily deal with one guy but he was calling up reinforcements! I started moving towards the sound because as he was talking my time was running out. I moved more quickly. The large vehicles the delegates were using were parked close to the exit in a group. He had to be there. I kept to the periphery and while I did I changed my gun for the Glock knife! If I had to use the gun it would make an appalling racket in the sound chamber that is this garage. If I had to silence this guy permanently it would be with the knife!

There he was, looking towards the doorway and then swinging round to view the rest of the space. He had the telephone to his ear and was talking quickly and quietly. I manoeuvred between the vehicles and circled round behind him and waited until he had hung up. I was on him before he had put the mobile in his pocket and he was down and out. I had hit him hard behind the ear with the handle of the knife I always carry with me. I disarmed him tied his hands with his own tie and forced his handkerchief into his mouth. I relieved him of his mobile, switching it off and putting the sim card in my pocket, it may contain interesting information that could be useful later.

Part two of my plan was going to have to happen very quickly and then I would have to go equally quickly! I rolled under one of the vehicles and loosened the brake fluid line. I repeated this on one of the other vehicles and then packed away my toolkit and returned to the entrance. I knew there may be FBI guys galloping to the garage but rather than run away and invite a chase I felt that I could brazen it out and make my way back the way I had arrived. I hurried through the doorway and along the corridor but instead of keeping to the main route I went back via the laundry as I had arrived.

"Oh!" exclaimed a young girl coming out of the laundry as I was passing.

"Sorry," I said, "Just taking a short cut!" And hurried on!

In two minutes I was back in the Reception area and ordering a coffee to read with one of the morning papers, which were strewn around the low tables. I had no intention of staying long but I needed to be anonymous and unhurried. It was only 07:15 and so much had happened already today. The main lifts opened into the foyer on my right. I was facing the main entrance. The lifts opened and out stepped our party, guards/FBI first followed by the politicians the rear being brought up by more guards. They went out through the revolving doors to the waiting vehicles. There were five politicians where at Harvard I had seen six; my emetic had done its work!

I allowed the party to leave and went out to collect my hire car then followed an approximation of the route they would take to Harvard. It was only a short distance, a matter of three or four miles, to the university. After a couple of junctions I observed what the Americans describe as a 'fender bender' had occurred at the next set of lights. I pulled in to the side of the street and took out my mobile. I stood at the side of the road as if taking a call with my mobile and photographed the scene. It was chaotic! As it happened the vehicle that had failed to stop and had run into the back of a regular citizen had been the last in the caravan. The others had made it through the lights and continued on. The two delegates and their guards were stood on the pavement while one of the party was trying to pacify an irate driver who'd had his car damaged. They were doing their best not to pull the FBI ticket and draw attention to themselves!

I'd taken some good shots that would be soon winging their way to the media! There was nothing more to do in the States so I decided the sooner we returned to Salem and reversed my route out of the country the better. It was a palendromic journey, that is, as slow out to Salem as it had been in to Boston the first time that I had taken the route. It was late morning when I arrived at the Amelia Payson. I asked the owner for my bill and went up to my suite. Surprise! Surprise! No sign of Naomi. I sent a text to Sumisu and Naomi to say that I was returning to England. I forwarded on the photographs I'd taken with the comment – SUCCESS!

I packed my bags and checked the rooms to ensure that nothing had been left behind. After a final sweep I went to the Foyer, paid my bar bill and left what in fact was a day earlier than planned! I'd been booked to fly from Boston to New York and then back to the UK. I decided on the driving route for anonymities sake and it meant I could still make the New York flight. After a fond farewell with mein hosts I set off back west towards Buffalo. I had not gone a hundred yards when my phone chimed to say that I had a text message. I pulled over and as I did so I glanced in my mirror. There was a car pulling away from the hotel that then pulled in as I did. Shit! The message was from Sumisu and simply said, *'Take Care!'*

Damn, he had got wind of something and I was being followed. Assessing the situation I realised that the hire car was no good anymore and nor was travelling to Buffalo. I decided to drive back into Boston and dump the vehicle. I liked the idea of the crowds to get myself lost in! I made no attempt to lose the tail I had picked up. I drove to a multi-storey car park in the centre of the city and dumped the car. I wiped it clean of prints inside and unlike most Americans I took the stairs instead of the lift! The company I had acquired didn't enter the car park so I was expecting them to be watching the exits, which wasn't the brightest plan because they would not know where I was exiting. On the other hand they may not be that worried because Patrick A Steele would not be able to get on any aircraft in the USA without being picked up.

I messaged Sumisu '*Spotted will take alternative route*' in fact there is only one direction that I could take and that would be north into Canada. The trouble is that the FBI will know that as well so it is down to me to be as inventive as possible in making my escape.

I took the opportunity to change my clothes while I was in the car park, to my black hoodie and trainers, and pocketed all that I felt necessary, which consisted of arms, passport, money and my Samsung Galaxy Tab. I went to the exit of the car park and strolled out as if I had all the time in the world. I left the holdall, clothes are easily replaced. Even though it was a dull day I had put on sunglasses so I would look a little different from when they had seen me earlier in my business casual garb. There were a number of people about but only one wearing the usual 'uniform'. He was staring straight at the door that I had just exited and at first did not spot me but I saw him do a double take as I turned away from him. He obviously wasn't sure because he didn't tail me. I followed the sidewalk signs for the City Centre and headed that way walking quite quickly. The only places I was sure of were those around Harvard and The Charles Hotel. I needed to grab a train timetable. There was a germ of a plan forming in my mind. I knew I would not be able to leave the country by air; no it would have to be overland. I also felt that it would have to be via Canada, and as secretly as possible. But I required a timetable to be able to plan my journey!

Initially, I strolled into Tommy Doyle's, ordered a coffee and took a window seat. While I was drinking I was thinking that Patrick Steele needed to disappear from the USA as soon as possible!

The pretty blonde waitress that I had spotted earlier came to wipe my table and top up my coffee.

"Is everything ok sir?" she trotted out as easily as breathing.

"Fine thanks. Can you tell me where I can find a train timetable honey?" I asked.

"Sure sir! I think I have an old one out back. Be right back!" she countered.

Two minutes later I was perusing the said leaflet. The plan I had was not feasible. There was no direct rail link into Canada from Boston, I would have to travel via New York or maybe I could return to Buffalo, it is only a short walk over the bridge across the river into Canada. There is another advantage. A train leaves at 21:25 tonight and arrives in Buffalo at 02:20 tomorrow morning. I obviously would not be able to cross at that time but I would try and find a tour group crossing the river to view the falls from the Canadian side and cross with them in the morning.

I had plenty of time before the train was due to leave so I decided to do some shopping. I needed luggage, a weather-proof coat and a change of day clothes. I walked out of the coffee bar and was bade farewell with the customary, 'Have a nice day!'

To which I replied,

"There is a tip under my plate!"

I found a huge TK Max and did my shopping there. They have a reputation for 'cheap and cheerful' clothing and I did not want any attention drawn to myself and it was crowded. I used cash - that would have to be the order of the day – cards are so traceable. I found a restaurant and ate sushi with chopsticks and then made my way to the South Station. I bought a ticket and paid extra for a business class seat that would allow more legroom and headrest so that I could get some sleep.

I needed to get a message to Sumisu. I decided to do this in two stages. I messaged *'Is she safe?'* and then I tried *'Going to see the Mounties riding Buffalo tomorrow at twelve'* I don't know whether I had been clever enough or too clever but all I could do was wait for a reply. I didn't have to wait long for the reply that indicated the message was understood and said *'See you there!'* Thank God! I made my way to the platform and boarded the train even though it was an hour to departure. Having done this before I wasn't surprised that the train felt damper and colder that the air outside. At this time of year it was very cold at night and today was no exception. I pulled my new weather-proof coat tighter round me, plunged my hands deep into the pockets and shivered. At that moment there was no one else in the carriage, I could see quite a way down the platform and there was nothing that worried me.

After half an hour or so I felt the carriage vibrate, the lights flickered, went out and then came on and stayed on, and the heaters started working. It was 21:00. There are a few others on the train now - in the cheap seats! I had no fellow travellers in my carriage. I think I am going to be lucky! We set off bang on time, unlike at home in the UK, and I kept alert. A uniformed steward came along and asked me if there was anything I wanted. I ordered coffee and a biscuit, which he brought back fairly quickly along with a blanket. Always worth paying a little more – I gave the almost mandatory 15% tip and off he went happy. I couldn't risk drawing attention to myself by being overly generous, or the opposite!

Sleep came to me fitfully. The motion of the train making it easier to drop off but the lights and noise kept periodically waking me! Still the five-hour trip went well and almost before I knew it I was disembarking into the freezing night air on Buffalo station. Thank goodness for that and as far as I could see no tail and no reception committee! I'd bought a small suitcase with wheels and dragged it along the platform following the few dozen people exiting the train. I had seven or eight hours to kill but booking in at a hotel was no option, as I would have to register my passport. It'd be risky enough using my passport to get into Canada. My idea of crossing with a tour group would hopefully make it less so!

The coffee bar on the station concourse was cheerful enough so I went in there and ordered hot drinking chocolate – I was fed up with coffee – and began reading a cheap novel

I had picked up at the travel shop. It was quiet but not totally empty all of the time, people arrived on and off throughout the rest of the night and so I was not too conspicuous. It was so cold! At 07:30 I left the station and found a MacDonald's that served breakfast. It was quite busy even at this early hour. I ordered a breakfast muffin with bacon and a fried egg (over easy!!) and sat down to replenish the flagging energy resources of the inner man. While I was eating I spotted a sign for tourist information and planned to go there next. I wanted to pick up a group as quickly as possible. I took a couple of free coffee refills and killed over an hour by the time I got up to leave the café, which then was busy. I strolled to one of the revolving stands and picked up a brochure for a visit to the Niagara Falls and looked at the times of the tours. There was one for the US side and the Maid of The Mist! In fact they were the only ones I could find. I decided to go in and speak to a member of the staff.

    The only one that was any good was setting off at 10:30 and was the full monty! A trip on the US side, down on to the boat then back up for the crossing over the river into Canada over the Niagara Gorge Bridge for a trip up the Skylon Tower and lunch, returning to the US side by 14:00. It wasn't cheap either! Still I booked a place hoping there was going to be a sizeable party. I'd a little time to kill so went and did some window-shopping buying myself a woolly hat and some gloves. Well it was cold and the hat would change my appearance!

    People started gathering about fifteen minutes before we were due to set off. Judging by the sizes and ages of some of the others on the trip we wouldn't be doing anything too strenuous. There weren't so many of us, only around eight to ten but still easy enough to detach or embed myself as the need arises. I stayed as much in the background as possible, being pleasant with my companions but not enough to be memorable. A small blonde girl in a semi-formal uniform of navy skirt, white jumper with red scarf came to round us up and introduce herself as 'Kathryn – your tour guide'. I'd never seen so many white teeth in one mouth! She took us to a minibus and off we went on our quite informative journey. The girl was efficient and patient and not in the slightest bit as 'sugary' as I thought she was going to be on first meeting. In fact she was very knowledgeable and attractive enough to be around, if I only had more time!

The only down side was the ride in the large lift down to the Maid of the Mist. We shared it with another similar party that was being led by a loud-mouthed pillock called Dwayne who was trying to quote poetry to Kathryn and impress her. I didn't see anyone in either party that wasn't embarrassed including Kathryn. It took me back to the time when I rather injudiciously 'smacked' a man who was being a pain in my local before Sumisu and the art of Aikido tempered my usual reactions. Still it would have made me feel better if I could silence him. Must not draw attention to myself!

We 'did' the boat trip, which turned out to be better than I expected, and then returned to the top of the gorge ready to cross the bridge. Now I felt the adrenaline start to flow. This was risky! Kathryn had us all on the minibus in minutes and had collected passports to show at the Canadian border. We travelled a few hundred yards and the bus pulled up and Kathryn went into the prefabricated building that was the passport control office. She was away five minutes and came back with one of the officers. He checked everyone including me and returned our passports. I kept an eye on him as he walked rather hurriedly back to his cabin. Come on Kathryn get a move on I thought! I had this feeling that there would be a reception committee when I got back to the border crossing, apart from the fact that I wouldn't be there! Another thought crossed my mind, and that was that they may not wait, the CIA operate abroad! Once we arrive at the Skylon Tower I would be taking my leave!

We went up in the express lift and walked round the viewing deck with the sections of glass floor and then headed for the restaurant where a communal table had been organised for us with a set menu. I was beginning to wonder if Sumisu had received my earlier message! We were about to sit down when I spotted a familiar face - Naomi Kobayashi! I excused myself saying that I must go to the bathroom. I headed away and caught Naomi's eye and indicated that she should follow me. I continued until out of sight of my party and then turned to Naomi,

"It's good to see you Naomi san!" I said with a slight bow.

"And you **Patrick** san," she blushed.

"We need to get out of here. The FBI is certainly on to me and I think there was some kind of warning at the border a few minutes ago. The CIA will be after me if we don't move." I related all of this in a hushed whisper.

"We have plans Patrick. It may be a good idea to get out of this vertical cul-de-sac. It would be so easy to trap us here!" she said.

"Bloody hell!" I swore, "That is the only reason they let me through the border! Let's move quickly. Link arms with me Naomi!" I instructed.

    We walked quickly to the lift and once inside I fastened up my coat and put on my woolly hat. She was wearing a long brown wool coat and pulled it tight round herself, then took some sunglasses from her pocket and donned those. We made quite a striking pair at almost six foot tall and smartly dressed. When we got to the foyer it was busy. There were people milling around, another party entering and some men trying to push their way passed stationary groups of people. We continued ignoring the guys coming in and looking for the fellows watching the door. We went into the souvenir shop that was inside the main entrance and started to peruse the goods on sale while surreptitiously observing our only escape route. There were two obvious 'problems' out front! We waited until there was a significant number leaving the Skylon Tower and followed on.
    As we exited the building one of the guys started walking towards us and I was preparing to act when an extraordinary thing happened. An elderly gentleman collapsed into him. I was about to go to help, as were others when Naomi pulled me away and we left rapidly placing a large parked vehicle between us and the front of the tower.

"What are….?" I started.

"It was Sumisu!" she hissed. "We have a car – come on!"

She guided me away from the Tower keeping something, a vehicle, a tree, people, between it and us! As soon as we got to the car she set off.

"Wait a minute Naomi!" I shouted. "What about Sumisu?"

"It is planned Patrick," she said in a matter of fact manner.

"But how will he get away? We should help him!" I insisted. Naomi smiled. "He is like smoke Patrick! Have you never noticed how he just appears when he needs to see you? Well he can disappear just as readily!"

"I must find out how he does that and get me some!" I commented. "So where are we going?"

"You will see very soon Patrick." She smiled and set off in a direction that would have us driving on deeper into Canada.

The route we were on was heading north and I fully expected that at some point we would turn east towards Ottawa. I said as much but she just gave me that enigmatic smile and we continued on our way. After a couple of hours she pulled into a roadside cafe and we swapped over. We were on the western shore of one of the Great Lakes.

"Keep the lake on your right!" was the only clue as to our destination.

"We are heading for Chippewa International!" she stated. "Without stops we could be there by 01:00 tomorrow morning. But we will overnight in a Holiday Inn near Crawford. It is called the Super 8 Grayling!"

I had driven for another couple of hours when we arrived in Crawford. We checked in, booking a twin room, and then went on the road to an Arby's to eat.

"A twin room Naomi!" I commented.

"Do not get any ideas Patrick san!" she had reverted to the formal.

I smiled and she sneered back! We ate part of the massive meal that the waitress put in front of us paid and left.

"This is an excellent escape route Naomi. I'd have headed for Ottawa!" I said. "And probably have been apprehended!"

"Yes well Sumisu is good at disappearances!" Naomi said again.

"I'm beginning to realise how good." I said.

We went back to the hotel and went to bed, each in our own double bed! I was woken the following morning by the sound of the shower. It was 07:00 and she was totally appetising and looked very refreshing in the almost inadequate hotel towel. I tried not to stare and went to use the facilities myself. She was dressed by the time I had showered and shaved. We made our way down to breakfast.

"What now then Naomi?" I inquired over the muffin course.

"We go to Chippewa International Airport and fly back to the UK."

She replied simply.

"What about Sumisu san?" I asked.

"We will see him later, at your home." She said.

"I have never heard of Chippewa, which airlines fly in and out? Do we have to change at another airport to complete the journey?" I demanded.

"You have so many questions Patrick. We are travelling in luxury in an executive jet courtesy of the Gurentai. The airport provides a customs service so Canadian officials will check us out." With that she fell silent and concentrated on driving.

We had a couple of hours to travel and although we did not encounter any difficulties we were both very watchful. We arrived at the airfield, calling it an International Airport was rather over egging the pudding, at lunchtime and the jet was waiting for us. We headed straight for the plane. The customs guy was chatty and overtly friendly. He looked at our passports and I stayed very still. I was ready to take him out if he got awkward. He gave them back with a cheery,

"Ok – have a good flight!" and then he left.

"You were going to hit him weren't you Patrick?" Naomi asked.

"If I had to!" I replied.

"I could sense you tensing like a coiled spring." She stated. "Aikido teaches us to move into action from a seemingly normal attitude!"

Thinking about it I don't know what that would have gained because to the best of my knowledge the pilot may have refused to take us as well and I can't fly and I don't think Naomi can. We would still have been stuck. We'd have had to consider a different course of action but if I had attacked the customs guy it would have made life considerably more complex. I need to learn to think more effectively and more quickly – use my Aikido training properly. That is why Naomi sensed my tendency to recourse to action as a first and a last resort!

"Yes Naomi, I need to use the Aikido mental exercises more effectively and be less impulsive." I said ruefully.

She pantomimed a round of applause!

"Where are we flying too, if I may ask?" I demanded.

"Manchester!" was the response. "We arrive around midnight UK time but it is only around seven and a half hours in flight."
The plane was very comfortable, normally a 12 seater but the inside had been gutted and a lounge created. There was the

captain, a co-pilot and a stewardess all of Japanese nationality. Why was I not surprised? Their English was impeccable but as far as I was aware they were not Gurentai. Naomi confirmed that so to the crew we were simply rich kids on a jaunt to Europe! Better to not let them think anything differently.

The flight itself was good, trouble free, well catered and relaxing. It was an opportunity to get to know Naomi a little better and also for her to learn more about me. We had an hours Aikido meditation and gentle exercise led by Naomi and we also ate, Japanese food followed by warm sake. After a couple of hours sleep we would be in Manchester but first I got in touch with Bill Fordyce and asked him to meet us in the Jaguar at International Arrivals at the airport.

It was wet and cold in Manchester but thankfully we were soon on the way back to my apartment with Bill driving. Once we got back we just crashed out for the remainder of the night.

We were woken with a cheery,

"Good morning Patrick!" from Stacey as she came through the door.
I was asleep on the sofa and Naomi was in my bed. I could hear Stacey pottering around in the kitchen, the kettle boiled and her footsteps took her into my bedroom. I had to smile to myself. I don't know what Bill would have told her but the exclamation I heard when she took the hot drink into Naomi made me smile. She came into the lounge and found me in my shorts and said,

"Did you have a row?"

I laughed.

"We are not in a relationship Stacey but Naomi is a good friend and someone I work with," I explained gently.

"Oh! I see," then in hushed tones, "Is she Mr Sumisu's daughter?"

"No. The company I do most of my work for is Japanese and we have been in the US together," I said.

"How long is she staying then?" Stacey asked.

"I don't know," was my honest reply.

Sumisu arrived shortly after we had dressed and after his customary Green Tea he started to de-brief us on the trip we had just completed.

"I have circulated the information you sent back from the USA to the media in this country and copies to our colleagues in France and Germany. The reaction has been variable. In the political press there has been comment about the unlucky nature of the talks and the fact that key delegates have been missing at important times due to a string of seemingly unconnected incidents. There have also been comments on TV along similar lines with speculation that these talks were not meant to be. The reaction from Finance Ministers has been overly zealous in the denial that there is a problem! There have been no publicised plans to reconvene the talks at present. In short Patrick there has been some success!" he concluded.

I really didn't know how to feel. Yes we had been successful, nobody had died, and doubt had been put in the minds of the politicians. However, the area that may just ensure that relations were on a more realistic level with the USA would be if the population in general were galvanised into action.

"Yes Sumisu and thank you for your assistance. The thing is what do we do next? I don't feel that the job is finished. We have to get the ordinary people involved in anti US protests!" I insisted passionately.

"We will help as much as we can Patrick and it may be that what you have done so far may find its way to the two political extreme parties in the UK!" commented Sumisu.

"UKIP and BNP?" I said quizzically.

"Yes. You seem sceptical Patrick." He re-joined.

"Well they are not held in particularly high regard Sumisu san. The BNP because of the associated violence and racism, and UKIP for their blatant ineffectiveness! Also UKIP are very anti Europe so they would be of no assistance in establishing stronger links on the continent." I explained.

"That is true but all you require initially is the driving force to energise the British people against America." He countered.

"I want to set up a meeting with both parties, separately, and explain what I think is happening and asking for their support." I said.

"If there is anything we can do to help Patrick," he said with a smile.

"Well I would ask that you or Naomi or both come to the meetings with me. If I am on my own it will have less influence." I requested.

"Let us know the date, place and time Patrick and we will organise something?" Was the more than generous reply. With that, formal bows and a peck on the cheek from Naomi, off they went.

Chapter 7

I had a few days rest and relaxation - after the intense nature of the time in the US I needed it! My Swiss account was very buoyant when I checked it and there does not seem to be much of a relationship between what I do with what I am paid. The apartment on the same landing as mine became vacant because of the death of the occupant and, so that I could have more control over my life including the desire not to share the access to the street or have someone else so close to my personal space, I had made an offer that my deceased neighbours relatives were not about to turn down. I had plans for the extra space. I want to turn my little flat into a more luxurious apartment!

Some of the time off I spent with my buddies and I also rekindled my fitness training and Aikido sessions with Vince Thompson. For the first time I felt a certain emptiness when I thought of Naomi and Sumisu. Still that may not be for much longer. Chatting to my friends I discovered that an acquaintance at church, Harry, has a son who is a bodyguard for the leader of the BNP – Nick Griffin. That would be my way in and I would send Mr Griffin some information via this lad.

I went to the annexe and found not only Vince Thompson but also a spotty youth I took to be Stacey's nephew - Ethan Small. He was on the cross trainer. Bill came to meet me as I walked in,

"Hello Patrick. I hope you don't mind Ethan being here."

"No it's ok Bill. Let's see how it goes," I replied.

In fact I was feeling invaded. I like my own personal space particularly when I am training or developing my Aikido. If becomes a nuisance I will move him on. I have no objection to him using the place but not when I am in. I'll tell Bill later. Everything was absolutely as it should be. Bill keeps the place immaculate and the kid had done some painting so that felt a little better.

I did some research on the Internet and found that there were articles about the various problems that the Americans had experienced both in the UK and back home. I also checked out the Foreign policies of both extreme parties and neither had a statement regarding the US! That I found quite revealing in itself! They were all worried about our financial commitment to the European Community and the rules that were imposed upon us but had no inkling of the real threat to our sovereignty. Well maybe they needed a push in the right direction and then we, as a nation, would wake up.

The danger in involving BNP is the violence of which they are capable and my ability to control this factor. I don't wish the campaign against the US discredited in the eyes of the populace. No there needs to be a program of anti-American marches, protests at their public buildings and the military bases in the UK. They have a considerable number of military personnel in this country, which is a worry in itself.

I spent the next few days putting together a portfolio of what I consider as possible proof of US intentions. It consisted of photographs taken of the delegates going to meetings; the Gun Law being pushed through Parliament; the size of the US military capability in the UK, and the apathy of our population and their willingness to accept anything the US say as gospel. I also included evidence of the actions I had taken already, both in the UK and America and my aims for the future. Because of the nature of the policies the BNP and UKIP have towards Europe I did not include my intention to align us more closely with France and Germany.

Once the information was pulled together I had a word with Harry in church on the following Sunday morning after the service. After the initial chat we had I approached the subject of his son and his work. To start with he was a bit defensive, Griffin's reputation is such that many people think that he taints all within his sphere of influence. As I pointed out to Harry, his lad is freelance and not employed personally by the BNP just the security firm he works for. So after not much persuasion he agreed to ask his son to pass on the envelope!

The next step was to contact UKIP, a much sterner proposition. After a little research I discovered that we had a branch that is quite local to where I live. Certainly within the nearest ten miles! The chairman is a man called Jason Smith and he lives in the highest town in England, Queensbury. There are pubs and restaurants in the area! I need to start frequenting these locals and see if I can 'bump' into Mr Smith! This could be quite pleasant, getting paid for going out socialising. It wasn't going to be that difficult – God Bless the Internet – I have pictures of Jason Smith and his address. Thankfully I have no intention of causing Mr Smith any harm but it would be so easy with the information that is freely available online!

The next evening which was a Friday, I drove up to Queensbury, which only took half an hour from home, and started to circulate the locals. There weren't that many! Of course there was no guarantee that he would be out drinking, he could be out with his wife or staying at home. The first place I tried was The Village. It was every bit as parochial as it sounds! The décor was jaded 70s as were the clientele, who were conspicuous by their absence. There were only half a dozen folk in the dingy place! I ordered a glass of beer, which was rather insipid and slightly warm, and sat at a corner table and took out my Galaxy Tab that I had brought with me. The idea being that I could photograph the customers if necessary. I also had a download of some books on the device, in case I got bored! It was approaching 21:00 and one or two more people had walked in but none of them looked like Mr Smith and nor was there any lively banter about local politics, or anything else for that matter. I waited until 21:45 before drinking up and moving on to the Ring O' Bells about 75 yards down the road. It was considerably busier than The Village, there would be no opportunity for photography but I did get a bar stool at the end of the counter in a position where I could see people coming for drinks and entering through the main door. The tables were all full and it was noisy but, because of the no smoking laws, the atmosphere was not too fetid. There were groups of people standing chatting, drinking and laughing, but no sign of my quarry. I had one more glass of slightly better quality beer and then left for home.

  When I arrived at the flat I felt frustrated and dissatisfied with my progress. I opened my favourite malt whisky and sat down, gazing at the dark outline of the hills from my lounge window and pondering directions and alternative strategies. I decided to repeat the exercise of going up to Queensbury but this time I would email Jason Smith and ask to meet him concerning the UKIP Foreign Policy and the USA. It could do no harm, as he doesn't have any inkling of who I am, what I have done and also of what I am capable!

There was no time like the present so I issued my invitation to meet over a glass of beer in the Ring O' Bells on the following Sunday lunchtime at 12:00. It would give Smith a couple of days to reply and me the same length of time to consider my approach to him. My initial thoughts were centring on the spurious possibility of becoming a member of his organisation. I wanted to quiz him about the real possibility of the UK being absorbed into the US. I didn't put the last bit into my email; he would probably dismiss me as a crank.

I was pleasantly surprised to find an email from Jason Smith in my Inbox the following morning. He would be delighted to meet me and possibly recruit me into UKIP. Great news!

The next couple of days I spent training, keeping fit and scanning the media for some reaction to the information I had sent to the British National Party. So far nothing was happening and I was wondering whether Griffin had received the information I'd sent through his bodyguard. It could be that they needed a push in the right direction! I also kept popping in to my annexe to observe Ethan Small. I was beginning to consider the possibility of employing him, but as yet hadn't decided in what capacity.

Sunday morning I went to church as usual to have my sins forgiven! Afterwards, instead of going to the local, I set off up to Queensbury and my meeting with Smith. I decided to dress smart but informal and to travel in the Jaguar in an effort to appear more desirable as a future UKIP member. It only took twenty minutes and I was in the pub with a drink in front of me when Smith arrived. I knew him immediately from the photograph on the website. It was obviously an old photograph! He was altogether rounder and more florid than I had expected. I rose and walked to meet him as he headed for the bar.

"Mr Smith, what can I get you?" I asked.

"Oh! Ah. Mr Steele?" He stumbled and nodded, "I'll have a G & T if you don't mind!"

"Not at all Mr Smith." I replied pleasantly even though I was thinking that he enjoyed the opportunity of the free drink! When he was served I continued,

"Shall we sit over here?" I indicated a table in the corner by the log fire that was roaring away.

It is amazing how changing one feature in a room can totally alter the character and ambience! It was warm and welcoming and somehow 'older' than late on the Friday night of the previous week. I was watching Smith guardedly while we settled ourselves and had an initial sip of our drinks. I waited to see how he would start. He glanced down at the table and then straight into my eyes and asked outright,

"Why would you want to join our party?" in a friendly enough tone.

I spent five minutes or so explaining my feelings about the dilution of our culture and the need to engender the English culture into our young people. I had brought a copy of the portfolio I had put together and it was on the seat next to me in a plain brown A4 envelope. I saw Smith eyeing it and obviously desperate to ask what was inside. He would find out when I was ready for him to find out!

"Mr Smith I am looking to tie my allegiance to an organisation that reflects my concerns about the future of England!" I stated. "That could amount to a considerable level of financial support. However, I need my ideas, which by the way are supported by evidence, taken seriously." At this point I patted the envelope on the seat next to me.

"So what is it that you are referring to Mr Steele? What are you giving us that constitutes 'evidence'?" he demanded.

"I have checked out your manifesto, particularly the Foreign Policy, and you are missing a huge area of influence on our country. That I find frustrating." I said exasperatedly.

"What is it Mr Steele?" he asked again more gently.

"Do you realise that there is a foreign country out there that is having a suffocatingly huge influence on our culture and your party have no policy in reference to this country?" I stated. "Do you know where the danger to England lies?" I went on, "Do you seriously believe that our problems come from the EU? Oh yes! They have an excessive influence on our financial behaviour, but they will not change our culture in the long term." I paused.

"I am sorry Mr Steele but you obviously have an obsession about something that I am not aware of. Now I appreciate the drink but I am not altogether sure that UKIP is the organisation that can assist you or that would benefit from you being a member. On that note I think we should take our leave of each other." He remarked pompously.

Before he could go any further I picked up the envelope he had been eyeing so avidly and said,

"In here is a collection of real evidence and information that will support what I am talking about. If I am to join your party I need to know that it will take my suggestions and ideas seriously. I will warn you now that it will require a change in your party's attitude towards some countries in Europe." I finished.

"What is in there?" he demanded huffily.

"It outlines the current situation and possibilities for the future and the actions I have already taken to slow down the influence of the USA on the UK!" I left the statement in the air giving time to Smith to think about what I am saying to him.

I passed the envelope over and sat back taking a sip of my drink, observing Smith as he became more fascinated with what I had given him to read.

"Would you like lunch Mr Steele?" he asked.

"I must refuse Mr Smith. I need to be elsewhere but I appreciate the offer. What I suggest is that we meet again in a week when you have had time to read what I have given you if that is ok with you," I stated with a smile.

"Ok Mr Steele! Here in one week's time," he agreed.

I finished my drink, stood up and left.

It didn't seem like a week later that I was in the same place at the same time with the same person! He had also brought back the information I had taken him previously. I wondered what he has made of it. He didn't seem any less enthusiastic and was equally happy to accept the G & T as before.

"What do you do for a living Mr Steele?" he began.

"Why do you need to know Mr Smith? Does UKIP only take people from certain occupations?" I countered.

"I saw you drive into the car park in your Jag!" he replied.

"I'm an accountant Mr Smith," I said after a pause.

"Whom do you work for, if you don't mind me asking?" he persisted.

"I have my own private business Mr Smith. I only handle single, high value accounts and work solely on personal recommendation," I explained.

"Oh I see!" he commented. "I just like to know how serious our applicants are Mr Steele."

"Almost the truth Mr Smith. What you really mean is who on the membership are likely to be major contributors!" I said sarcastically.

He had the good grace to look embarrassed.

"I must apologise Mr Steele. Regarding the information you gave me it is all quite plausible but the US are our friends. They have supported us for years over a number of issues," he stated.

"Mr Smith if you are not interested just say so. I have spent considerable time over a number of months collecting and collating evidence and I am happy with my conclusions. Are you prepared to feed this through to your executive committee for consideration or are you going to remain Euro sceptic at the expense of our country being ceded to the Americans as a result of negligence and apathy?" I asserted.

"I have spoken to one or two people and they are considering what you have presented but there is no doubt our main focus has always been Europe," he responded.

I drained my glass and stood up to leave.

"One moment please Mr Steele. I've ordered lunch, I thought we may talk in greater depth!" he said with some consternation.

"Give me a reason to stay Mr Smith!" I ordered.

"Mr Farage is interested in what you have collected and is discussing with other senior figures what, if anything, we can do as a party – publicly," he replied.

I sat down again and Smith went to the bar and bought me another glass of ale. We chatted about the state of the country for a little while longer until the landlady called us to go through to the dining room for what turned out to be a well-cooked but plain lunch. During the meal we talked more closely about my findings and Smith agreed, superficially, with where I was coming from. He wanted to know about the type of activities I'd been involved in when we got on to the 'accidents' that had befallen the US delegation both in the UK and on their own soil. I explained that I have a wide and varied skill set including marksmanship, Aikido and bodyguard training, some of which had been useful in the last few weeks. Smith looked shocked,

"I don't think we could get involved in any kind of physical action against the States Mr Steele. We have to consider the reaction in the country. We are a serious political party and would not enjoy being a laughing stock!" he commented.

"I understand what you are saying Mr Smith. What I require is political support in the asking of questions of government and shadow cabinet ministers. I need questions asked at the European Parliament regarding the US role in Europe and the rest of the world. I need your marketing machine to target the older end of the population, who are more likely to support your overall cause, and include some of the glaring evidence of a US take over in the UK. It will be harder to gain support from younger people who are less aware of what English culture is about," I explained.

"Ok Mr Steele. What do we get out of it if we do as you ask?" Smith requested.

"I am not so naïve as to think that the party will not require some sign of loyalty and commitment. What I will do is make a donation to party funds and I will pay for any publications containing material supporting my position as long as I have the opportunity to vet what is being printed." I stated. I sat back in my chair having finished my lunch and looked at Jason Smith and waited for a reaction.

He sat quietly for a moment then looked up at me and said,

"I haven't the clout to be able to give you an answer immediately Mr Steele but it would seem that your membership would be no problem and a donation without strings would be great, however only the exec can ok what you are suggesting," he said apologetically. "Personally, I can see merit in what you are postulating but I am sure you will agree that it's a major policy shift for us!"

"Yes of course. I'll give you my card with contact details and I will expect to hear from you next weekend Mr Smith. Thanks for lunch. Bye!" I rose, shook his hand and departed leaving the poor guy pondering the future of his party.

When I was at home in my apartment I thought about my request and its ramifications. I'm sure I'm just the same as the majority of people – blessed with afterthought. Had I asked for enough or was it too much? It would be interesting to see if they get back to me! I do feel that what I have asked for would be of positive assistance to my cause and ultimately the benefit of the nation. I am assuming of course that is what most people want – to maintain our independence and sovereignty. It would be awful to wake up one morning to find that our taxes were going to the US and we answered to some second rate movie actor or the like. To me that would be the pits!

The following day I went down to the annexe after a half hour run and did some weight training followed by a session with Vince Thompson.

"Vince," I began, "How are you getting on with Ethan?"

"Ethan. He's ok!" said Vince briefly.

"Is that it?" I laughed.

"Well no not really. He is a feisty lad, got a bit of a chip on his shoulder. He works hard when he is in the mood. He learns quickly but I get the feeling he would let you down if you expected reliability," Vince stated.

"Ok thanks very much Vince! Are you happy to continue to work with him?" I asked gently.

"Yes he is progressing but he hates practising," said Vince.

"Great!" I replied seriously. "Thanks Vince."

I was thinking that perhaps Ethan, if he is interested and measures up, could work for me, doing some running of errands, tailing people and the like. Just a thought!

I didn't have to wait until the weekend! Two things happened that really surprised me. Jason Smith rang to say that the Executive Committee of UKIP is going to meet to discuss my concerns on Wednesday, two days hence. The second occurrence was a letter pushed under the door from BNP, I assume pushed under by Harry Shellford's son. It was not what I was expecting! It just said:-

'Thanks for the information. We will get back to you. Watch this space!'

It was not at all clear what they intended from that brief missive. So things were moving on both fronts as I wanted them to, so far! In the meantime I was beginning to consider if there were any other steps I could take to maintain the momentum I had established by action in the last few weeks. The proposed Gun Law in itself would not make us part of America; it was more a symptom of what could happen. The finance committee seemed to be temporarily in abeyance, whether as a result of my actions or as a result of some hiccough in the negotiations, I don't know. There are so many simple things that present themselves as targets but that would not have a significant effect on my campaign. Bombing MacDonald's and the like would be a dead end. No I would need something that effects central government.

There are a number of US bases in the UK. One of the biggest is at Mildenhall east of Ely in Cambridgeshire. It is an 1100-acre site housing 10,000 people. The current might of the UK armed forces is numbered at 194,440 personnel. They have 5% of our personnel on one base! When you consider we have military people stationed in various parts of the World, they have more than enough people at Mildenhall alone to make a serious assault on our government.

On top of that most of the US bases are known and referred to as 'RAF', for example RAF Menwith Hill, RAF Lakenheath, and RAF Feltwell whereas in reality this is not the case. At the larger US bases there will be a US Commander in post who is in firm control and occupation. In other cases, at a base like 'RAF' Feltwell, for example there is no RAF personnel present and it is the US Commander who decides who has access to the base – as does the US Commander at all such bases.

The land occupied by the US Visiting Forces and their Agencies is in the possession of the Secretary of State for Defence they already have control of parts of our country. The US authorities own all the buildings and infrastructure. On many of the bases they are a complete 'US entity' with a school, leisure facilities, supermarket, a medical centre, church and housing for US families and military.

Where there is an RAF presence there may be a contingent of staff, along with an RAF Liaison officer who is ostensibly in charge. There may be a Ministry of Defence Police Agency (MPDA) presence too. The MPDA have limited powers and are paid for, and under the operational control of, the US authorities. In short we have no power in certain areas of our own country! There is even a group called The Campaign for the Accountability of American Bases or CAAB for short! I'm not the only person in the country who feels similarly. I need to galvanise a group into action against what the Yanks hold in this country already.

I have no issue with ordinary American citizens they are exactly the same as ordinary people in England, but the manipulation of equipment and land by those in power, is an entirely different question! It may present me with some other opportunities to upset the Yanks. That may turn out to be a job for the BNP, in the way the 'Ban the Bomb' lobby worked in the 1960s. They could also add a touch of belligerence and destruction to their campaign, which could actually focus the media attention on what is going on in our own country! I liked that idea very much!

Wednesday came and went and I continued my training regime but with my thoughts on the UKIP meeting and its outcome. I felt that I had put myself in a position to use them as the legitimate anti-US group and the BNP as the more 'active' group. Obviously they could never be seen to be working together, but what the eye doesn't see the heart won't grieve about, and I'm certainly not going to tell either party about the others role! What I was waiting for came the following day in the form of a call from Jason Smith. I knew straight away that the news was going to be good just from the tone of his voice, all chirpy and overly cheerful.

"Mr Steele?" he began, and after I had confirmed and we had exchanged pleasantries, "I am pleased to be able to tell you that the Executive Committee are going to include, as part of our Foreign Policy, a section on managing relations with the US. Also we are prepared to produce a flyer, at your expense and with your veto, at reasonably short notice for circulation in areas of the country chosen by yourself with advice from our marketing people. In fact, as I speak, there is a small working group meeting to begin the design of the flyer. I hope you don't mind but as you have the right of veto I thought it was sensible to start as soon as possible," he concluded.

"That is good news indeed Mr Smith. Thank you," I replied. "I am sure you will be in touch when you have something to show me."

"Yes. Er! Actually I've been asked to request a deposit Mr Steele. I hope you don't mind?" he said.

"Of course I don't mind Mr Smith. Would £1000 be enough?" I countered.

"Well that is quite a lot but if it's ok!" he stammered.

"I will have a cheque in the post for you tomorrow and if you don't mind I would like an update every week at the very least Mr Smith," I demanded.

"Certainly Mr Steele I will see to it personally. Speak to you soon, Bye!" and with that he hung up.

  I sat back in my red leather-covered recliner and smiled quietly to myself. Obviously, UKIP are after the money, but the fact that they have taken my proposal on board legitimises my judgement of the situation and is the first step in the battle to maintain our independence. 'Yes I am well pleased' I thought to myself. 'Very well pleased!'

  It would be asking too much that BNP would be as easy to negotiate with! I produced a cheque for Stacey to post and I wanted Sumisu and Naomi to know how things were going so I messaged them. I received an answer from Naomi, which simply said '*See you tomorrow*'. I wonder what that's about I thought?

I went to the Annexe in the office and found Bill and Ethan there.

"Hello gentlemen!" I said heartily. "I hope you aren't too busy."

"Why is that Patrick?" countered Bill with a smile. Ethan just looked sullen.

"I've had a letter this morning to say that the solicitors are completing the purchase of the next door apartment and I have plans I would like the two of you to help me with." I said. "Ethan!" I continued, "Would you be interested in a more formal job for the next few weeks?"

"Doing what?" he grunted.

"I'd like you to work with Bill on the apartment. I'll pay you minimum wage with bonuses and see that all is legal and above board. The number of hours you work are up to you but I must have a minimum of 16 per week. To start with the bonuses are – the use of the gym facilities, when I am not here; Aikido lessons with Vince, which are compulsory and for which I will pay you and a tax-free financial bonus when each task you are given is completed satisfactorily." I explained.

Typical youth he stood scuffing his scruffy trainers on the floor before he begrudgingly replied with a barely audible grunt.

"Thanks Patrick!" smiled Bill, nudging Ethan. "Stacey will be really pleased. Come on Ethan!"

"Thanks Mr Steele," he said pleasantly enough.

"What I want to do is to put a second door at the bottom of the stairs, and to convert one of the bedrooms to an office," I outlined, "The kitchen I will keep in my apartment but I want a dining room and a games room in the new property. The bathroom in my flat can be taken out and I want to use the space as a hi-tech communications centre. I will have an en suite added to my bedroom. Any ideas you two can come up with round my requirements would be greatly appreciated."

"That sounds great Patrick! Thanks again," he said glancing at Ethan.
I left them to make their plans and to contact Stacey, and Ethan's family.

Chapter 8

A couple of days later I received a letter from the BNP. They wanted me to meet someone predictably called 'Smith' in Dewsbury at a supermarket café next Wednesday at 13:30! I couldn't believe it! How cloak and dagger can you be? I went on to their website for contact information and in all honesty it was sketchy when you get down to analysing what it contains. There was a London telephone number, and an address in Powys, Wales; and a further contact address in Nuneaton. No other name appears on the site apart from Griffin's until you delve deeper and come up with another MEP – Brons! Hardly surprising that this meeting is so covert in nature! Ok I'll play their game to achieve my own ends.

Wednesday came and I made sure I was in the supermarket early! They arrived, yes there were three men, and they wore jeans, sweaters and coats of different styles. One of them stayed at the door. He bought a newspaper and stood reading it leaning against the wall just outside the entrance. Scruffy, unshaven, about 5' 10'' and very thin! He looked tough, but there was also something about him that raised feelings of aggression in me. I think it was an arrogance in his manner and also a slightly worrying confidence. I could have happily walked up to him and decked him! Now that is not like me, I am usually very calm when metering out punishment. I continued after the other two men.

The supermarket was busy, Wednesday afternoon – aren't people at work? I watched the other two split up, one into the market the other to the restaurant. I waited until the time reached 13:37 by my Rolex and then strolled into the cafe. It is like all these places, washable floors and table tops, bright and clashing! Every noise jarred the nerves! He was sat at a table by the window at the back of the room so that I would have to sit opposite him. He looked quite tall, it is always difficult to tell when someone is seated, and he was broad across the shoulders, clean shaven and with small piggy eyes. I saw him glance at his watch a couple of times, which is why I was intentionally late, to get him on edge. I took my time and looked vacantly round the tables until he raised a hand and beckoned me over to him.

"Hi!" I said smiling, "I am Patrick Steele," I held out my hand and he shook it a little too firmly!

"Bob Smith," he replied. "What can we do for you Mr Steele?"

"Have you read my portfolio Mr Smith?" I asked pointedly.

"Yes I have Mr Steele and frankly I don't see what your point is. The Americans are our friends and they have similar ideals to us around race, terrorism and religion. Why should we worry about them?" he stated in an abrupt manner.

Seems to be that arrogance is a prerequisite of membership!

I stared right back at him and controlled my breathing using the meditation techniques learned in Aikido. I kept my expression deliberately bland and kept very still. I could see him becoming more uncomfortable and there was something else – he was puzzled.

"That is quite disappointing." I said. I then went into a spiel about the military establishment of the US on our soil and our lack of control over their bases. "Can I ask you a question Mr Smith?"

"Certainly Mr Steele, fire away!" he responded in a friendly enough way.

"Would you like to be governed by the Yanks Mr Smith? Would you like to have to pay for your Health Care? Would you like to have to sell your house if you or a member of your family became ill? Think about that Mr Smith." I asserted standing up and making to leave.

"Hang on Mr Steele, no need to be hasty. We might be able to come to some agreement!" he rushed on. "I just needed to know how serious you are."

"I am very serious Mr Smith and there may be some financial support for your party if we can come to some kind of working partnership," I confirmed forcefully.

"What sort of ideas are you considering that we would benefit from Mr Steele?" asked Smith.

"The military bases concern me greatly. As I have said even though on some there is an RAF liaison officer they have no real say in what goes on at the bases. Places like Mildenhall with 10000 personnel and 1100 acres are totally autonomous. That number of personnel represents 5% of our military capability. If you said that there are similar numbers on three or four other established bases then we are talking about a medium sized army on our own soil over which we have no control! I would like us to cause as much disruption, legally, as we can. A little like the 'Ban the Bomb' demonstrations of the sixties and seventies! The Yanks will not be expecting anything so some broken fences and sheep wandering on to their premises, I am sure you can make something up. It must look like peaceful protests about global warming or the like but I must stress no criminal activity above trespass," I concluded forcefully.

"It sounds interesting Steele but how much money are you prepared to donate? I have to go back to the Exec with some type of carrot!" he said.

"The money side will depend on the quality of your workmanship but I will say that I have set aside £10k for the purpose at present that is not a limit! To set the ball rolling I would like you to come up with a plan to cause disruption at RAF Menwith Hill near Harrogate. It's not large and is mainly involved with satellite tracking and communications. See what you can think of that will satisfy my requirements," I instructed. "Now I must leave." I left him a business card and walked away purposefully.

I'd parked my car, the Renault, in the town centre at the back of the Civic Hall by a meter, about ten minutes' walk away from the supermarket. I kept an eye open for a tail as I walked steadily into the town and sure enough the guy who was left outside the supermarket was about fifty yards behind me. I walked a little quicker and when I got to the back of the Town Hall I nipped round the corner and found an alcove that would conceal me quite well. It was the entrance to a rear door sheltered by a wall about ten feet long and six feet high. The door was at the end. I waited until he rounded the corner took a couple of steps passed my hiding place and stopped swearing audibly. He'd lost me! Rather than give him time to think about where I could be I whacked him between his coat collar and woolly hat with the side of my hand. I caught him before he dropped, pulled him into the lea of the wall and left. By the time he'd roused himself I would be half way home! I didn't want my car identified and as a matter of principle neither did I want some over enthusiastic thug knowing anything more about me than was necessary.

The following day I'd just finished breakfast, Stacey was cleaning and I was contemplating when Sumisu would arrive and would Naomi be with him when there was a knock at the door. Stacey mustn't have heard because the knock came again. I checked the door camera and was surprised to see Ethan standing there. I opened the door and he looked like a startled rabbit.

"I thought it would be Aunt Stacey Mr Steele," he stammered.

"It's ok Ethan, come in, she's in the kitchen." I said kindly.

"Actually er Mr Steele I wanted to show you something," he said gaining a little confidence.

"Ok Ethan come through and sit down!" I instructed.

He stood for a moment and then pulled a rather creased roll of paper out from somewhere inside his coat. He spread it out and put it on the coffee table using coasters and candles to hold it down. He then launched into a pacey description of what I was looking at.

"It's a plan for the changes that you want to make in here and next door Mr Steele. Aunt Stacey let me in for a look round. See what you think," he said.

I looked at his ideas and was quite impressed. He had some unique suggestions. I said,

"Ethan I really am very impressed." I indicated some parts I liked and some things I wasn't sure about and went on, "Can I have a look at this until the weekend and I will let you have it back Saturday?"

"Yes. Sure. Thanks Mr Steele," he smiled.

He was going to roll it up again and I stopped him. I wanted him to leave it where it was so that I could keep glancing at it. He seemed pleased at that, he is obviously a lad who is struggling with his own identity. Well I hoped what I have done so far has helped. He popped into the kitchen to see Stacey who, I felt sure, knew what had been happening! I heard the door slam shut and a couple of minutes later, while I was looking at the plan I felt a hand on my shoulder and received a tearful peck on the cheek from my domestic assistant.

"Thank you so much Patrick," she said.

"It's fine Stacey. The lad has a talent," I replied.

Another knock at the door while I was pointing out what Ethan had planned. This time it was my Japanese friends. Stacey left to make drinks, she was used to two coffees and a green tea by now, and I greeted the pair of them. The next two hours were spent apprising Naomi and Sumisu of what had happened so far including the plans with UKIP and BNP.

Sumisu had news for me from Europe and the contacts within the media that he seemed to be able to rely on. Apparently, the French and Germans are following our activities quite closely. I suggested that they relay the information about the military bases in the UK. Probably more relevant to the Germans than the French!

"It seems that you are making some significant progress Patrick," stated Sumisu. "The plans you have put forward are very good if they come to fruition, which they seem likely to. Is there anything we can help with Patrick?" he asked.

"It has crossed my mind to start making some inroads into the other US bases. I have thought to move quickly and decisively, causing property damage and inconvenience as well as stirring trouble up in the local communities!" I explained.

"We would be of no assistance to you if we were seen, however, low level covert work would be a possibility along with providing equipment," Sumisu concluded.

"That would be greatly appreciated Sumisu san!" I responded. "Perhaps Naomi could accompany me and liaise where necessary. A couple staying in the local hostelry is less comment worthy than a guy acting on his own." I commented.

"I would be very happy to help you Patrick," responded Naomi. "When do we start?"

I was pleased and I think she was too. I continued,

"I would like to start by visiting Mildenhall in Suffolk. It is a very big base and the town and surrounding area have a number of pubs and restaurants that we could use to upset the Americans. It's also close to Lakenheath so we could kill two birds with one stone!"

"When do you intend that we leave Patrick?" asked Naomi.

"I am expecting to hear from Jason Smith at UKIP in the next couple of days and then we have the weekend. Shall we leave on Sunday?" I suggested.

Naomi responded with,

"I will see you Sunday at 09:30 Patrick."

After another few minutes of chat and a list of the equipment we would need the two visitors took their leave.

The following day, Thursday I received a call from Jason Smith of UKIP to say that he was posting a draft document to me for distribution and would I proof read it and send it back. I said of course and if it arrived before Saturday lunchtime he would have it back by Monday next.

I prepared myself for the trip south by exercising and then loading the Renault Espace 2011, with my Swiss OM 50 Nemesis sniper rifle and silencer, and Glock handgun with knife. I packed a holdall with my night kit as well as a suitcase with smart casual clothes.

Sunday came round quickly and the tall and elegant Naomi Kobayashi arrived as arranged and we set off on the long drive to Mildenhall. It always seemed to me to be a long journey travelling to the south east. We continued our pattern of driving, two hours on and two off so that we were comfortably in the area by mid-afternoon. I'd studied a map beforehand and, after much thought, decided it would be preferable to stay in one of the villages a little away from Mildenhall and Lakenheath. I'd also been considering what strategies to use and to an extent believed that the actions of the BNP may dictate at what level I entered the fray! However, I had no indication of when they would begin their action in Harrogate so maybe I needed to pre-empt what they were going to get involved with by some significant assault on one of these two bases. The horns of a dilemma!

I had the idea that the minor sabotage indulged in thus far was precisely that - minor! One of the alternatives I was currently considering was, for me, quite extreme. The airfields have aircraft landing and taking off quite frequently and they would make significant and expensive targets! That is one of the reasons the sniper rifle had been included. I am able to hit quite a small target from a mile away, which would reduce the risk of capture.

Naomi also has a myriad of skills as well as hand-to-hand combat. She is expert in setting explosives and booby traps and is also a good long range shot. She had brought her own equipment and I was beginning to think that a multipoint attack would create greater consternation in the minds of the Americans. I relayed my thoughts to my companion and she concurred. It would also create 'news' in the country and that is what we are looking to do. We concluded that I needed a date from the BNP but first we must book in to a hotel.

We eventually decided upon Worlington Hall Hotel, a three star in the village of Worlington about a mile and a half away from Mildenhall and about four from Lakenheath. It's an elegant 16th Century former Manor House set in five acres of grounds. It offers the full facilities of a Country Hotel: á-la-carte restaurant, function suite, lounge bar, gym, swimming pool and charming accommodation. The original house was built in 1570 and the Queen Anne façade was added in the early 1700s, when it was turned into a manor house. Now it is a distinguished Country House Hotel with signs of recent restoration reflecting its original design. The building is listed as being of historic interest, set in five acres of land, useful for jogging, that leads down to the River Lark.

We booked a twin room in our names and planned for a stay of a week. The use of our own names is not an issue because we are not tied to any organisation neither do we have criminal records that would raise our level of visibility with the authorities. Having said that if we do get caught our cover is blown and we need to remove ourselves very quickly, however, we have no intention of getting caught! We were both happy to share a room and our relationship was very much that of brother and sister. We seemed to be very close, however, and there has been some friendly physical contact. Naomi is very much more 'touchy feely' than I am. Typical reserved Englishman! I didn't object to having this striking, raven haired, Asian lady hanging on my arm. Who would?

We decided to have a drive around the area in an attempt to orientate ourselves and then returned to the hotel. I messaged the bogus Mr Smith of the BNP asking when they would hit Menwith Hill in Harrogate. I also contacted Mr Sumisu and told him of our plans and the idea of hitting three bases at the same time. I was surprised at the response that came back to me, which was *'why not hit four?'* Of course, I had forgotten that Sumisu san was also a highly trained field operative. There were two other bases that we could attack but the one that was most tempting is RAF Croughton, it's a United States Air Force communications base in Northamptonshire to the southeast of the village of Croughton. The station is home to the 422nd Air Base Group and operates one of Europe's largest military switchboards and processes approximately a third of all U.S. military communications in Europe. If we could organise a breakdown in their communications that would be a significant blow to the Yanks!

I conveyed my thoughts to Sumisu and he said that he would 'organise something' for that base! I was very pleased about how things were coming together. Over dinner that evening Naomi and I chatted about our plans and I particularly wanted to know what Sumisu would be capable of doing.

"Patrick!" started Naomi with an amused expression, "Sumisu san may be somewhat older than us but he has a full set of very well developed capabilities. It was Sumisu who taught me about explosives, Patrick, and I wouldn't be surprised if it is explosives he uses against the base at Croughton," she concluded.

"I see. He is also a considerable adept at Aikido, as we both know. Disrupting their communications would be a first rate strike coupled with what we are doing and not forgetting the BNP." I replied.

"Yes Patrick. By the way," she said sarcastically, "what are we going to do?"

"We are going to shoot down a couple of their aircraft!" I stated cryptically.

"I beg your pardon Patrick!" she countered.

"We are going to set ourselves up with the sniper rifles and we are going to deflate the tyres on one of their aircraft at each base." I said. "What I suggest we do tomorrow is find suitable places to set ourselves up and spend time watching the activity on the bases."

"Sounds good to me Patrick!" She replied.

  The remainder of the meal was spent in pleasant and relaxed conversation and in anticipation of the action to come. After a short walk to help settle the meal we turned in for the night. It still felt weird to me that I was sleeping within ten feet of a good-looking Japanese girl and we were not making love! We were on inactive service!
  The following morning I got up first and went to use the hotel's gym facilities, showered and then went down to breakfast. Naomi joined me a few minutes later and just as she sat down my phone emitted the receiving message signal.

It was from BNP. *'Tomorrow'* was all it said. I passed my phone to Naomi and she forwarded the message to Sumisu.

"Patrick, it doesn't give us much time to get ready." stated Naomi.

"Let's finish up here and get started." I suggested.

Ten minutes later we were on our way to Lakenheath. Looking at the map three sides of the air base were too well populated to allow a would-be sniper to set themselves a hide for a shoot. The southeast was open land, rather flat but with some patchy tree cover. We made for a small lane about five hundred yards from the perimeter of the landing strip. It was pretty good. There is a sharp bend at one point and on the left in the 'elbow' of the bend a parking place. Just above that there is a small grassy knoll with a little tree cover. We got out of the car and walking hand in hand like two lovers we strolled up the hill into the bushes! Once hidden from the road we looked across in the direction of the airfield and sat under a tree and watched the activity for an hour or more. Planes took off and landed frequently. Aircraft of every size and shape but particularly fighter trainers! They were not such good targets, as they wouldn't create a big enough reaction. However, twice in the hour larger transports landed and there was one fighter jet. They would be ideal, particularly the fighter because they are so very expensive!! Targeting something like an A-10 Thunderbolt 11 or an AC 130 Spectre Gunship would be great, but if it had to be a C-5 Galaxy transport then that would have to suffice. The A-10 is relatively vulnerable as it has a single offset front nose wheel so one clean shot and that would cause an accident hopefully without injuring the pilot, but if that does happen – collateral damage!

So, decision made, we strolled back to the car and set off towards Mildenhall, a drive of about ten minutes. Once in the vicinity there were very few places that seemed to lend themselves to this type of covert operation. At the eastern end of the runway there is a huge area of managed forestry and a couple of old factory units. They didn't present the best shot but it was considerably closer than a mile so swings and roundabouts! I would find something suitable amongst those units. Okay then we had our sites set all we needed to work out were the logistics.

"I think we'll be up and off at around 06:30 in the morning Naomi and then if you drive the Renault, drop me off first and then go to Lakenheath. We take our shots, you return and collect me. How does that sound?" I asked.

"You don't mind me driving your car Patrick?" she queried sweetly.

"Not at all Naomi as long as you don't do any damage!" I replied.

"That seems fine to me Patrick," She responded. "Shouldn't we be taking our shots at around a similar time?" she went on.

"Good idea Naomi. If we have our mobile phones on we can coordinate," I replied.

So plans set we returned to the hotel and did tourist things like any couple in love. Hand in hand full of smiles! The weather was not brilliant and the forecast for the next day wasn't particularly good either. As long as we had a few minutes in which to take our shots that shouldn't be a problem. In fact if there were a drop or two of rain it would keep potential nosey parkers out of the way. We went back to the hotel and after dinner had an early night.

We were up at 05:30 the next morning and dressed in our warm dark clothing. The sniper rifles were in the hidden compartments in the back of the car in my holdall and, in an anodised case was Naomi's. It was still dark being early November, and that fact gave us cover for getting ourselves in position. The journey itself was not going to be a long one but we would probably have a lengthy wait for flights to start. There were regulations about flying at night in built up areas! We were also driving through a light drizzle that would soak us once we were out in it and that also may cause problems for pilots and their aircraft. We both had quality lightweight waterproofs in fact Berghaus Paclite Jackets, which are windproof, waterproof and very expensive.

"We should aim for around 10:00 for our targets Naomi and then a quick text when you can come and pick me up." I smiled.

"That sounds like a reasonable plan," she responded with a grin. "Although I do think we need to take the first opportunity that arises. If the weather worsens or the US has different plans we may not get another chance!" she speculated.

I mulled that one over in my head, immediately realising that she was correct, and agreed,

"Okay! You're right of course!" I concurred rather ruefully.

We arrived at my place and she kept the engine running while I collected my rifle in its shapeless carrying bag. No point in giving people clues as to what we are about, not that I was expecting to bump into anyone. Once again I received a kiss on the cheek as she turned and got back into the car with a cheery but hushed,

"See you later. Keep in touch by text!"

"I will Naomi," I smiled.

Off she went in my car as I turned to slip into the cover of the woods. First obstacle was a barbed wire fence round the trees. As I remembered, the copse is managed and I shouldn't have been surprised. Using a fence post I vaulted the barrier and was at once knee deep in soggy undergrowth. I moved into the trees and circled round until I had arrived at the front edge nearest the airfield that was no more than four hundred yards from the runway. I moved slowly and quietly using a mini maglite torch to find my way through the darkness of the trees. It wasn't that difficult as being managed the great plants were well spaced and for the most part kept clear of undergrowth. That in itself was a double-edged sword - undergrowth provides cover! Still I would be angling my shot upwards more than likely so I'd keep low.

In the meantime Naomi had arrived at her hiding place and parked the Renault in a convenient cart track. Her site was a little more elevated, around 35m above sea level, which may not sound much but according to our map the airfield was no more than 7 or 8 metres above. She had the opportunity of a range of shots. The easiest would be similar to mine in that if we waited until the planes touched down it would be a steadier target. However, for me, without the benefit of height, I would probably have to hit the wheel when the plane was above the ground. Naomi found herself a slight hollow that would keep her body below the general ground level, and provided a support for the 'legs' holding her instrument.

Neither of us was particularly comfortable and would need a hot shower when we had done but with Aikido the mental ability to separate the mind from the discomforts the body was suffering was well developed to the point, in our case, where I wasn't even shivering. That will be very important when about to take the shot with the Swiss rifle. We would also have to use silencers so that our risk of detection was further reduced. The sky was lightening although not by much as a result of the persistent drizzle, but at least there was sign of an improvement over in the east where it was possible to discern the lighter shade of grey where the sun would rise at 07:34, according to the local TV news we'd watched on the equipment in our bedroom.

An hour later and nothing! The text that came from Naomi suggested that she was having a little more luck in that there had been a take-off of a Galaxy transport. If we became desperate we would have to target something taking off. If we hit the nose wheel before rotation was achieved they would skitter into an ignominious crash. I texted that information to Naomi! She came back with, '*After 14:00 first available target*', I replied with a simple agreement.

As luck would have it we did not need to wait for too long. Fortunately the drizzle had eased to the occasional sensation of dampness when I heard a distant whining roar that was being magnified. I didn't have much time so I lined up the muzzle of my gun with a point over the runway nearest to me that should be about 50 feet above the ground. I had my eye to the telescopic sight I wouldn't have much time. The sound of the plane was increasing rapidly to a cacophonous roar, this was no A-10 Thunderbolt it was another Galaxy C-5. The nose wheel on these things has four tyres that would need to be punctured, four shots! The massive black shadow appeared overhead and seemed to travel away from me in slow motion. I had to aim at where the wheels would be rather than where they are and I had to start firing immediately. I emptied my lungs and rather than pulling the trigger I squeezed off the first shot, levered the second into place and fired again and then twice more. I could see I had hit the target, even though I say so myself, I had no doubt I would hit what I aimed at, I always had in the past! I dismantled the weapon and removing the sight first so I could watch the result of my handiwork. I watched the great, grey behemoth sink to the ground as if nothing had happened. The rear under carriage began touching down at first as gently as a feather. It travelled seventy five yards further before the nose started to drop gracefully and as it did I felt a bubble of excitement. The tyres hit the tarmac and for a moment nothing happened. The plane was still travelling at around 150 mph when the tyres gave out and the shower of sparks from the metal rims created a display every bit as glorious as fireworks on bonfire night. The great plane started to slew round to the right and off the tarmac and as soon as it hit the grassy surround it seemed to try and tunnel under the earth like an enormous mole. The noise was astounding and the forward motion was converted by the clinging wetness of the earth into a sideways slide. There was turf, smoke and other debris beginning to blossom like a filthy cloud and then everything stopped. The Galaxy had come to rest at last, the engines were silent and nothing was moving on the airfield. Time seemed to standstill! Then suddenly there were sirens and people running and general mayhem. I completed the dismantling of my sniper rifle and returned it to the holdall, then withdrew further back into the trees. I had a ghoulish desire to stay and watch but I knew what I must do. I messaged Naomi *'Job done'* and then found a hide in an impenetrable part of the woods to wait for her message to say that she was on her way.

Naomi received the message and sent back a smiley face with the mobile and returned to waiting. There were one or two jet trainers that had taken off and landed and carried out the 'touch and go' manoeuvre that smartened up the pilots familiarity with their planes. She was deciding that it would have to be one of those little planes that would be her target as the longer I was in hiding the greater the risk to me. Periodically, Naomi flexed her muscles to remain supple and alert when she noticed a somewhat deeper note approaching from her right. She was at right angles to the runway and would have a clear view of the wheels. Luck was in big style; this was the A 10 we'd been praying for. Naomi slowed her breathing and turned her rifle towards the plane tracking its approach through her sight. She focussed calmly on the nose wheel and as soon as the rear wheels touched she loosed off three rapid shots at the front under carriage. The result was somewhat more spectacular than in my case. The plane had less under belly to protect it and so the noise and mess was much more violent. The pilot ejected and rose like an arrow into the misty sky. Immediately, she did what she had been trained to do, clearing up, packing her case and waiting for the fuss to begin. She also made for cover as quickly as possible. There was the slim chance that the pilot might notice her movement if she tried to escape when he started to descend. There is a small stand of trees close by that she made for and there she kept an eye on the pilot. He could be a problem depending on where he landed. His parachute had opened and because there was no breeze he was coming straight back down on to the airfield. All the attention was on him, on the plane and on the damage caused. At that point Naomi took off to where she had parked the car then sent me a text and set off back towards my spot. We were back in the hotel in twenty minutes, job done!

Chapter 9

After a shower, and no I did not get the opportunity to scrub her back, we went to lunch. We found a Go Sushi restaurant in Mildenhall and sat at the conveyor selecting the dishes we wanted and taking our time. There was method in our madness. The place had a fair smattering of Americans, both civilian and service personnel, and they were excited, you could tell by the volume of noise. We chatted quietly, eating and listening and also paying attention to the Japanese chefs who were working in the units in the centre of the conveyor. It was obvious that the Japanese were not happy to be serving some of their more voluble American clients from the comments, in their native tongue that we overheard. Much of the talk was about what had happened on the base a couple of hours earlier.
We continued to eat and listen. I received a text from Sumisu just saying '*Job done*' I held my mobile up for Naomi to read – she smiled!

"All we need to know now Patrick is have the BNP kept their part of the bargain?" she stated.

"Yes indeed Naomi. And do you know something?" I said.

"You don't trust them?" she responded quizzically.

"Exactly!" I answered.

"What do we do now Patrick?" she went on.

"What is there to do apart from return to Yorkshire and watch the outcome?" I smiled.

We finished our meal and walked out hand in hand, but it was rather like Egyptian policemen who walk down the streets of Cairo in the same way, close colleagues deriving a degree of comfort and trust from the contact. Naomi drove the first leg and we were home in four hours after a relatively uneventful trip. 'Relatively' because the news bulletins were full of reports 'just in' about incidents at four USAF bases in the UK! It would be interesting to read the newspapers in the morning.

We had not been away as long as originally planned so Bill and Stacey were surprised when we walked back into the apartment. I explained that business had been concluded more quickly than we originally thought. We hadn't been back an hour when Sumisu walked into the flat, led by Stacey. She was still nervous of him fumbling her way through an introduction. He smiled at her and said,

"Thank you Mrs Fordyce, most charming!"

She blushed deeply and left. Naomi and I both laughed, he was an old dog!

"Good evening Sumisu san," I said. "Have you had a successful trip?"

"Very much so Patrick. It will take some time for the Americans to unscramble the mass of plastic and copper that was once the main incoming junction box. They also lost some satellite dishes and power sources," he went on "Most enjoyable!"

All three of us laughed. The question is going to be what have the BNP been up to? We gathered round my computer screen and I started searching for latest news. Eventually we found a minor comment in the local evening newspaper about a demonstration at Menwith Hill on the outskirts of Harrogate but on the face of it in a low-key sort of way. I suppose we needed some bright young hack in a newspaper office somewhere to put all four of our events together and make eight! We would have to wait until the morning to gauge the response.

Sumisu and Naomi decided to stay over. The sleeping arrangements I was unsure about until Sumisu said,

"If you don't mind Patrick san, I will sleep on the futon down in the annexe and you two can stay here!"

"Ok Sumisu san, I will run you down there if you like," I offered.

"No need Patrick san, I know my way as long as I can take your keys and use the office while I am there?" he asked.

"Certainly Sumisu san," I bowed.

I gave him my keys and he left very quickly. We watched him strolling down the hill towards the road junction, which is the turn off into the industrial estate, and then he disappeared towards his destination. I went into the kitchen to make green tea and warm sake leaving Naomi gazing out of the window after the recently departed image of our mentor. I returned with a tray offering the beverages and we sat together drinking in companionable silence.

Naomi took hold of my hand after a little while, looking straight into my eyes and said quite unashamedly,

"Patrick, I think we should sleep together!"

Initially I didn't know what to say, but after a moment,

"It's what I want to Naomi." I replied.

She took my hand and we went into the bedroom together and sat on the edge of the bed. I put my finger under her chin, turned her face towards me and kissed her a long lingering kiss. We continued to kiss, more fervently now, then undressed each other and got into bed, as it was a cold night with the promise of frost by morning. Not something that I felt would affect the temperature in this bedroom.

"You are shivering Naomi. Are you ok?" I whispered gently.

In reply she kissed me again and we wrapped our arms around each other kissing more desperately than before and beginning to explore each other's bodies. She was firm and well-toned; her breasts were small, well rounded with dark nipples that were erect. Her bottom is incredibly firm and well-muscled. We collided together and made love, gently and with great consideration for each other. Afterwards we lay in each other's arms feeling warm and relaxed. We dozed and made love again in the night, this time more hungrily, and finally slept deeply.

We were awakened the following morning with tea and toast, English style, courtesy of Stacey, who delivered it in a charmingly embarrassed manner. Naomi smiled and in a totally uninhibited way leapt out of bed stark naked and gave Stacey a hug and kiss on the cheek.

"You are very sweet Stacey, thank you!" she said.

Stacey just laughed and scuttled off into the kitchen.

We ate and chatted for half an hour and then decided we needed to move. After showering, and getting dressed we walked down to the annexe where Sumisu was already up and about. In fact it was busy when we got there. Vince Thompson was limbering up on the dojo; Bill Fordyce was cleaning out the Renault, and Sumisu was sat at the computer screen in the suite of rooms that constitute office space and living accommodation. As soon as he realised we were there he called us into the office with,

"Patrick, Naomi come and see this!" enthusiastically for the normally reserved little gentleman that he is.

He was on the BBC website and found an article linking all four events. The headline was '**Accident Prone Americans**' and underneath a description of each event as it happened. The two plane crashes were enlarged upon because of the expense to the US, as was the explosion at their communications centre at RAF Croughton. However, the action at Menwith Hill was played down as an insignificant demonstration and included photos of some rather jaded looking people holding placards. The beauty of it was the signs said things like 'Yanks Go Home' and 'Give us our Land back'.

"This is excellent coverage Patrick," enthused Sumisu. "It would be even better if we could publicise the extent of their holdings in the UK," he went on. "Considering what we have achieved so far I believe we have the kernel of an excellent campaign!"

    I believe it was the best piece of selling that I have ever done and that from someone who would struggle to sell fridges in the desert. We now have to consider next moves and actions. And I was still expecting news from UKIP. I wasn't disappointed! Later the same morning I received a text from Jason Smith wanting to meet up as soon as possible! 'I wonder what's rattled his cage' I thought. If he has read the newspapers he will assume we have started without him! I messaged him to say the next evening at 19:30 at the usual place. Having relayed that information to Sumisu and Naomi they said that they would leave me to it because they didn't need to be identified by too many people.

"Patrick, we are both going to leave now. I will see you here at the weekend," she smiled.

"Ok Naomi, Sumisu san safe journey," I responded, and with that they left.

    It is strange but I have no idea where they go when they leave me. I suspect any family Takuo Sumisu has will have grown up and flown the metaphorical nest, but with Naomi Kobayashi, unless an orphan like me, she will have family to visit. She is obviously free enough to be able to see me. I like the girl a great deal but I am still concerned as to what type of relationship we can have if at all! There is constant danger to both of us in the work that we do and that would make a 'normal' kind of going on impossible. Maybe what we have now is all we can reasonably expect.

The following day I had a text message from BNP asking what I thought of their action and what next? I simply sent back *'more of the same, and that the photographs of the placards were great'*. In the evening I set off up to Queensbury to meet Jason Smith of UKIP. It had occurred to me that he may be getting upset if he thought that BNP were involved in the same plot as his party. Well they could like it or lump it that is the way things are! He was already in the pub when I walked in.

"What do you think you are up to Mr Steele!" he said as a preamble. He looked as if his blood pressure was up! His already florid face was a strange shade of purple.

"Good evening Mr Smith and how are you?" I asked pleasantly.

"Yes, oh sorry Mr Steele," he spluttered out. "I am ok but I am getting a load of earache from on high about who you may be getting us into bed with."

"That is something you have no need to worry about. What did you think of the occurrences of the other day?" I enquired.

"Well we know that there were four incidents at different establishments belonging to the US. Were you responsible for all of them?" he asked rather naively.

"If I tell you everything that is going on it will make you equally culpable. It is best that you don't know what you are not responsible for!" I retorted.

"Were you involved in the plane crashes?" he persisted.

"Suffice it to say that our plans are being put into place to protect the English people and culture. As things stand at the moment your party is in a great position of strength by not knowing what is happening right now. When your flyers' are being produced and distributed it will appear that you're responding, as your party should, to an invasion by a super power!" I explained.

Smith sat and considered what I had told him for a few minutes while I had a sip of my ale. Then he seemed to see where I was coming from,

"Ok, I see what you mean, so irrespective of what actually happens we are legitimising your position without getting involved in any 'action'," he concluded.

"Exactly, what you are doing is escalating the position to a legitimate level. It can only be good for your party," I ended.

"That sounds great Mr Steele. I hope you don't mind but I have been asked for an advance on the sum you agreed with me to start publishing the leaflets," he requested sheepishly.

I took out my cheque book and wrote him one for a sum of £5000 and handed it over saying,

"There you go, the rest when the flyers go out. I will need to see a proof please?" I stated.

"Certainly Mr Steele, I believe we will have that for you next week say Wednesday evening here?" he replied.

This guy seemed to know more than he was telling me but I concurred without fuss. I left shortly after that with him promising to hurry the leaflets along. I suggested that he Google US Bases in the UK, it makes some fascinating reading, particularly the sections that include the number of personnel, the impotency of our own forces to have any influence on those bases, and the sheer size and potency of the forces housed there. Notwithstanding the fact that they are called RAF bases but we are lucky to have a liaison officer stationed there. Almost an English ambassador on our own soil!

I sent a message to Sumisu and Naomi to say that everything with UKIP was ok. I received a reply from Naomi saying that she would be with me Saturday. For some reason I felt a tingle of excitement at the thought! Maybe it was those beautifully long legs!

In the meantime I needed to start planning for the next phase. We were just beginning to gather some momentum and it would be a waste not to further pursue what had already been set in motion. To a certain extent the choices were the same but the carrying out would be that much more difficult as the 'enemy' will be on their guard.

Saturday morning came with questions having been asked in the House of Commons regarding the problems that had occurred on the bases. At PMs Question time the incumbent responded that there seemed to have been some actions by a misguided and unknown group of individuals against our international friends and that a full investigation will follow! Now that is interesting, as it has caused a stirring at the highest level. The Americans had not responded in any way. The next steps must be more vigorous, possibly even more decisive than crashing a couple of planes. I'm thinking along the lines of BNP staging a sit in at RAF Croughton, the communications hub. Peaceful of course! Also Alconbury, along with RAF Molesworth and RAF Upwood are considered the "Tri-Base Area" due to their close geographic proximity, and interdependency, would be a very important target. It houses six squadrons—security forces and civil engineer, air base, medical services—and supports tenant units. It manages the daily activities in the community and maintains all facilities, services, and housing. Most importantly, its primary mission is support for the U.S. European Command Joint Analysis Centre. If we could upset their activities the benefits would be immense. It goes without saying that infiltrating would be tricky at the very least.

The campaign in the printed media must also be escalated giving information about the bases and our lack of sovereignty over them in our own country.

Saturday came and so did Naomi, and alone! A pleasant surprise! We tried to have as normal day as possible. I took Naomi shopping in Leeds and we had a meal at a Tapas restaurant at teatime before returning to my apartment. I walked Naomi through the new section and told her of the proposed alterations showing her a copy of Ethan's suggested plans. We then walked on to my local and had a few drinks with my mates before returning home to bed and another night of lovemaking totally without inhibition!

Sunday I got up and went to church leaving Naomi in bed. When I returned she was sitting in the lounge at the computer and researching information about the US bases in this country.

I kissed her on the cheek and said,

"Good afternoon Naomi!"

"Hi Patrick!" she replied, preoccupied.

"Find anything interesting?" I persisted.

"Yes," she replied, "the Tri-base Area.."

"Alconbury, Molesworth and Upwood!" I interjected for which I received a playful tap!!!

"So you have already seen them," she said with a wide grin. "And I suppose you have already considered the value of hitting them because of the strategic importance as support for the U.S. European Command Joint Analysis Centre!!!" she concluded.

"We think alike Naomi, or logically whichever the case maybe!" I responded.

"Logically!" she retorted. At which point we both laughed.

The following morning, Monday, Sumisu arrived at the flat and we discussed the next stage in our 'journey' concluding that we would hit the Tri Bases and send the BNP to RAF Croughton.

"Sumisu I would suggest that you make a nuisance of yourself at Menwith Hill! I understand there is a weekly demonstration on a Tuesday by the CAAB group!" I instructed. "You may be able to use the demonstration as cover! I would quite like to cause some damage to their radar equipment." I concluded.

"I will see what can be done Patrick!" he replied with a slightly amused expression on his face.

Sumisu would have to leave immediately as his job would be tomorrow night before any of the rest of us had started to work. That will not upset our plans. In fact if there is enough fuss created it may help distract from action at the other sites. I must contact the BNP and congratulate them on their work and re-direct their attention. I sent the bogus rep a text to say we needed to meet urgently. I received a caustic reply *'Tomorrow, same place, bring your cheque book!'*

The following day I left Naomi getting organised while I went to meet our friends from the BNP. I didn't take my chequebook I took cash. There was no way anyone was going to link me to that lot! I was there an hour early to avoid the gang that 'Smith' or 'Brown' or whatever his name is likely to bring.

"Hello. Have you brought your chequebook?" he demanded.

"I have brought some money." I replied.

We spent ten minutes discussing what they had achieved the previous week and what I would like from them this week. He didn't seem to have any objections.

"So how much have you brought?" he asked.

"I have brought £5000 cash for last week and a further £2500 for this week. I will give you the balance depending on results!" I stated.

"That seems fair," he replied.

"Now you'd best be on your way," I instructed. "After all you would not want any of your people to get hurt again, would you?" I finished.

He got up and left followed by two rough looking characters in jeans, coats and baseball caps. How naïve, or stupid, or both! I still didn't trust him. I found a small exit at the back of the store, through the warehouse, and left that way. I was home in no time and helped Naomi complete preparations for our trip to the Alconburies.

We set off the following morning after breakfast and drove south. To a degree our trip was the least well defined because we did not know what we were going to come up against. I had driven through the area on numerous occasions and there is nothing overtly different about RAF Alconbury and I had scarcely noticed the other two airfields. There was not even an indication that the US is in as much control as they actually are. We had packed C4, sniper rifles, timers and handguns as well as our hand-to-hand combat equipment. I was a little concerned with what Naomi and I could get away with. The area covered by the Tri-Bases is tight and, because of the JAC connection, probably well-guarded.

I was thinking like this while driving and, just after I overtook a car and caravan on the A1, it struck me what would work very well. Well I think so anyway. I pulled over into a Little Chef, parked the car, and sat staring out of the windscreen.

"What's the matter Patrick?" asked Naomi gently.

I sat in silence only dimly aware of the fact that my companion had spoken.

"Patrick!" she raised her voice a fraction.

"I am an idiot." I said. Naomi didn't disagree. "We need to change our plans!"

"What are you talking about Patrick?" she demanded with less patience.

"Do you remember the Wikileaks that have been coming out about all kinds of memos and emails between the US government and the rest of the world?" I asked.

"Yes!" somewhat tentatively.

"Well there was one centred around Cluster Bombs and their storage on UK soil!" I explained.

"Yes I remember it. There was something about a leading MP, finding a loophole that has allowed the US to store cluster bombs in the UK," she replied.

"Yes the brother of the leader of the opposition while the Coalition was in power under Cameron and Clegg," I responded somewhat cynically.

I went on and explained what I was talking about.

"On 03 December 2008 Representatives from more than 100 governments began signing a document binding their countries not to make, stockpile, or use cluster bombs. Many military powers - namely the United States, Russia, China, Israel, India, and Pakistan -- have declined to sign the ban. In fact Gordon Brown said his government will stop using cluster bombs. But the United States, one of the world's largest builders of the bombs, opposes a ban. A little self-serving I think," I concluded.

"So where is this leading Patrick?" Naomi asked.

"Well," I began. "If we can find out where they have stockpiled these evil weapons, maybe we can 'borrow' one or two, and take them away. We can photograph where we get them from and what that facility is like and circulate those pictures to all and sundry!"

Naomi smiled.

"Thank goodness Patrick. I was worried about what we were going to do," she admitted.

"Let's have a coffee and discuss our plans," I suggested.

We went into the café and ordered coffee. I took out my Samsung Galaxy ipad and searched for information regarding the size and location of these bombs. What I discovered was that they are approaching 10 feet long with up to 2000 bombs inside and weight between 400 – 500kgs. I had no indication so far as to where I would find them. Moving that size of load would not be easy and certainly would not fit in the boot of the Renault!

We were going to need a trailer and some kind of lifting gear. It would have to be assumed that there will be lifting equipment where they are stored, but I need to get a trailer as close to the storage facility as possible. One avenue that was not open to us was to blag our way in with some kind of inspection con! It would have to be a theft under the cover of darkness.

First things first I needed a trailer. Once again I used Google to find us a source of assistance and after only a few minutes I was hit with a perfect solution. A horse trailer; big and strong enough but totally at home on country roads! There were a couple of places near Peterborough and I telephoned the number on their website immediately spinning the yarn that my own vehicle had a broken axle and I needed to move my horse to the veterinary hospital for an operation on a twisted gut, and urgently. Fortunately, they had one available that I could collect this afternoon and it would cost me no more than £45/day.

I explained my idea to Naomi and we then started to address the next problem, which was to find a cache of these cluster munitions and then organise ourselves to steal an example, and finally to get away with it! Not too much to ask is it?

Using Google Map I searched for the airfields looking for aerial photographs and possible clues as to where there may be a storage facility. I began my search at the Tri-Base area, as that was where we were heading. In fact we struck gold almost immediately with RAF Alconbury. I checked out Molesworth and Upwood but they weren't big enough, however at the top of the runway and off to one side at Alconbury there is a collection of hangars. There were four of the great storage barns in total, three on one side and one on its own opposite, separated by a section of concrete large enough to allow aircraft to taxi. That would certainly provide the type of facility necessary, the question, were there cluster bombs here? We would have to get as close to it as possible and do some observing.

We had already been to Mildenhall and Lakenheath and they were operational aerodromes that may have a storage facility but on reviewing what we had observed hadn't spotted anything that offered such an option. Croughton and Menwith Hill do not provide a runway to allow for transport of the Cluster Bombs any longer so it must be Alconbury.

Having decided on the place, getting in and taking the ordinance would be a wholly different matter.

Chapter 10

We drove into Peterborough and collected our horse trailer and some other necessities, then continued on the short journey to the Alconbury area. The trailer was the usual zinc coloured, metal, rattletrap that they all seem to be, and slowed our progress as the maximum speed limit while towing in the UK is still 60mph! About three miles before we reached the airbase we found a lay-by and pulled in. It was getting towards dusk even though it was only 15:00 and I used the interior light so that we could see the ipad clearly. I had searched for aerial photographs of the environs and found something almost unbelievable. At the northern end of the airfield, just off the base and with an entrance directly from the road we were currently parked next to, is a MacDonald's! How typical is that? Also there is an access road directly from the base that does not look like it is gated or guarded in any way. I can't decide through arrogance or ignorance! I tend to believe it to be the former!

We decided on MacDonald's for tea! Hardly a gourmet meal! The restaurant car park is quite extensive and out of site of the dining room. Tall Leylandii surround the actual eating area but the car park goes back fifty yards beyond and behind the trees. The access road was at the furthest point from the restaurant building. I drove the car and trailer into the back of the car park behind the eatery, parked up and strolled into the garish eating space. We strived to find something edible, settling on something with chicken, that didn't taste too bad, then had superheated coffee and followed that with an apple slice at a similar temperature to the beverage. I really don't know how this particular chain of restaurants gets water over the temperature of 100 degrees Celsius! We were in no great hurry so we didn't burn our mouths! The plan was simple. We stroll into the air force base and have a look round! We then bring the trailer in and pinch a bomb and bugger off quick! Sounded easy enough and it began that way. We followed the well-compacted dirt road under a clear autumn sky that usually means, at this time of year, that there would be frost by morning. We saw no-one on the road until we came to a junction.

  I had a torch with me but was loathed to use it because of its attention grabbing qualities. We were very steady in our approach, listening and watching intently and arrived at the hangars within fifteen minutes of our leaving the car park. They looked to be in total darkness and loomed, like angular behemoths just waiting to pounce, against the skyline. We had just turned left when within 20 yards we arrived at the ribbon of concrete that separated the hangars. On my right against the dark sky were the three large, black hulks and on my left just the one monster! There was a path to our left that would wide enough for a vehicle and circles round the rear of the solitary hangar. On the right the buildings were all in darkness and silence except for our target. I felt sure that the solitary one would contain what we were looking for, but there was a guard strolling away from us towards the far end of the building. He wasn't marching but strolling and, judging from the red, intermittent spark-like glow, he was smoking. If he turned and came back when he reached the end of his patrol we would certainly be discovered. I pulled out my silenced Glock – just in case! We hurried off to the left behind the building the guard was looking after. I kept a wary eye on our patrolling soldier and he actually did turn and start back. We moved back into the shadows of some bushes that formed the perimeter and waited. The guy didn't come to the side or rear of the building he just patrolled the front. His must be a punishment detail. While I watched, Naomi went off and examined the back of the hangar, which only took five minutes. She came back and signalled that we should leave so we headed back the way we came and left the track after about 10 yards.

"There is a rear door but the main entrance is in front," Naomi whispered. "There is a light inside so I think maybe a guard room with other soldiers!"

"Right, we'll go back to the vehicles and rest up until 01:00 when we will return. At that point we'll bring the vehicles, you drive without lights and I'll walk in front with my hooded torch until we get to the final bend in the road where you'll stop and wait. We will then proceed to the hanger, immobilise the outside guard, enter the building and deal with whoever is inside there ensuring any communications ability is neutralised," I stated.

"Good plan Patrick. When we get inside I will move to the right and you to the left of the door and we will progress round the building until we meet at the far side," she added.

"We mustn't be worried about eliminating guards if necessary but it would be better if we can get through the night without killing anyone." I asserted. "We must not put ourselves at risk," I concluded.

On our arrival back at the vehicle we checked round to see that there was no one about and opened up the trailer. The hirer had insisted on leaving a bale of hay inside and we had put in the purchases we'd made earlier in the afternoon. All we needed to do now was to rest for four or five hours before we set off to do the dirty deed. I felt that we would do well as a team even though our experience of working together was limited. Naomi is a very able and confident person with a highly developed skill set and a strong personality. I set my alarm for 00:45 and after a drink of water and a nibble at some high-energy bars we set off.

We had prepared ourselves by donning black and gold Japanese Noh masks, stocking up with plastic garden ties, and arming ourselves with silenced handguns and knives. Already practised in Aikido skills we were very well prepared, we even had material for gags, and formidable. I had a walk round our vehicle and checked that all was secure. The restaurant was closed and apart from one other empty car the parking area was deserted. I checked the strange car out, the engine was cold and frost was settling on the windows, no one had used this vehicle for many hours. Just in case I deflated the tyres, using a matchstick, to prevent any possible future pursuit. Our Renault was warm in comparison and getting warmer, the diesel engine was ticking over quietly and the heater had cleared the misted windscreen. It was time to move although I didn't want to go out into the cold night air. Naomi jumped into the driving seat and engaged crawl gear in the automatic box and we eased our way out of the car park and on to the track that led to the airfield. I was still amazed that there were no guards or gates on this track but 'familiarity breeds contempt' and I was fairly sure the Americans felt that they were safe.

As I walked steadily in front of the car I was made more aware of the rumbling of the engine and the creaking and groaning of the trailer, all of which seemed magnified in the cold, clear, and silent night. We continued under the winter moon until we reached the final bend in the road and I signalled Naomi to stay where she was. I moved forward as silently as the gravel path would allow keeping to the grassy verge as much as possible for the sake of deadening my footsteps. I slowed and crouched lower to the ground so that my head would be below the top of the surrounding bushes. Keeping the hedge behind me, as that would give a black background blending in with my similarly coloured clothing; I waited until a trooper came into view from round the back of the hangar. I kept very still for a full five minutes before considering moving forward, waiting until the Yankee had almost reached the far end of his patrol before darting across the gap into the shelter of the hangar. I waited until his footsteps were back almost beside me, I heard him turn and set off away again, and I rounded the corner and hit him at the base of the skull with the butt of my Glock 17. I caught him as he fell and dragged him round the corner into the shadows. I used the garden ties on his hands and feet and gagged him as well. I went back to Naomi and beckoned her forward, eventually stopping her at the point where the track hit the concrete apron. She jumped out and we made our way round to the rear of the hangar - stealthily. Naomi led the way as she had recced the area earlier. I could see the light leaking out from around the doorframe and searched for the handle of the door. It was let into the metal so that it was flush with the rest of the portal. What we do not know is whether the door opens inward or outwards and that is going to be important. I approached the entrance and listened carefully but there was no discernible noise from inside. It had to be remembered that this is a big building we were about to enter and so there could be a full troop of airmen in the place.

I turned the handle and as silently as possible pulled on the door, as I felt in this type of building the space inside is at a premium. I was correct and it swung open noiselessly allowing a pool of light to wash out on to the rear of the property. Naomi went in and turned to her left and me to the right as we'd agreed. I closed the door and we both crouched down either side of the opening. It was quite an astonishing scene that was in front of us. The hangar is not unlike my annexe in that the whole floor space is uncluttered by internal walls but there is an office of some description in the corner to the left on the side nearest Naomi. The light we could see from outside was from a number of strip lights that were lit. They were not all on just enough to give safe passage between the serried ranks of racks that festooned the floor of the hanger that was now, to all intents and purposes, a warehouse.

At this point we had to be very careful because whoever is in this building will have communication with the control room of the base. I signalled to Naomi that we should start at the side we were on and sweep the whole floor before we approached the office accommodation. This we did at almost a run and found no one lurking around so we made our approach to the office in the corner. There were no lights on inside, as shown by the window in the end and the opaque glass panel in the door. We listened very carefully and could just make out some deep and regular breathing of an occupier, or occupiers, fast asleep.

Again we could not be sure what we would find so, same as before, I opened the door and Naomi went in with me following to the right. We stayed low and then waited. There were two occupied cots and a bit of a kitchen area. We moved to the men, who were dressed in shorts and t-shirts, flipped them face down, hit them on the back of the head, and tied their hands and feet before gagging them. They saw nothing! We checked the rest of the accommodation and found no one. I discovered radio equipment and just turned it off before disconnecting the mains and failsafe battery supply of power. I signalled to Naomi to come back in to the hangar with me. We were moving quickly but I felt more relaxed although we had to be watchful. The most hazardous part of the journey was yet to come! We had to identify the cluster bombs and remove one without being discovered.

The bombs have a serial number all of which begin with 'CBU' and have a range of numbers after them going from '52B' upwards. They all have a variety of types of 'bomblets' inside ranging from softball size intended to shred and dismember human bodies to those that have a dual role of dismemberment and fire starting capabilities! Nice!

We started to examine the racks nearest the loading doors so that we would not have far to transport the beast once we had identified what we were looking for. Inside the door there was a forklift truck that was obviously intended to move them. Really it wasn't difficult to find what we were seeking. I sent Naomi off to bring the trailer to the front door of the hanger. We had no choice because the bomb could not go through the rear door, besides it would take too long. I also asked Naomi to position the vehicle so that we could drive straight out of the base.

While she was away I went back into the office and found a key cupboard with a few sets of keys but only one lot that resembled car keys. I checked on the 'prisoners' and apart from being rather annoyed they were alive; I went back to the forklift and started it up. It wasn't too noisy being electrically operated, and I manoeuvred the thing into position by the first CBU-97 Sensor Fused Weapon and slid the forks either side of the bomb. There is a sling between the tines of the truck to carry the evil looking, torpedo shaped weapons. The bombs were secured on the racks with curved wooden blocks, which we would need to take with us to keep the bomb stable in the horse trailer.

  I ensured the straps were in place under the bomb then an inch at a time lifted the bomb enough to take the weight, around 500kg, on the forklift. I then went out of the hangar via the front door to wait for Naomi and our transport. My heart was now racing to the point that I felt it was trying to beat its way out of my chest. I was sweating even though the air temperature must be zero or below. I didn't open the main doors but exited through a small personnel door to the right of the main doors, closing it behind me. Naomi was creeping off the track on to the concrete apron and I watched her start to swing the vehicle round when everything went pear-shaped. A Jeep came screaming round the corner from the direction of the camp carrying two USAF armed troopers. I knew they were armed because the passenger was holding his weapon out of the vehicle window and pointing it in Naomi's direction. They screamed to a halt, jumped out, stood with legs braced at the front of their vehicle and indicated that Naomi should stop. Shit! I shrank back into the shadows and went into a crouched firing position. I didn't want to kill them that would reduce the effectiveness of our campaign. I watched while they indicated that Naomi leave the Renault. She stepped out and had their full attention. Well she would! Wearing her tight black leggings and sweater with the Noh mask completing the ensemble, she looked extraordinarily striking.

"Well what have we here!" said one of the Yanks.

Naomi didn't respond.

    I moved rapidly from my hiding place and circled round to the far side of the Jeep and approached the guy who had been sat in the passenger seat and rapped the speaker on the back of the head. He went down like a sack of potatoes! The other soldier glanced away from Naomi for a second and that was all the time she needed. She kicked the gun from his hand and hit him on the bridge of the nose with the heel of her hand with such a force I heard his head crack against the bonnet of their Jeep before he slithered to the ground. We tied them up, gagged them and left them in the back of the Jeep anchored to some struts that strengthened the sides of the vehicle. Naomi completed her manoeuvring and we dropped the tailgate. I continued my operation with the bomb moving more rapidly because I didn't believe that the two soldiers had arrived by accident! Getting the bomb in the trailer was not that difficult but securing it was more of a problem. I spread the bale of hay across the floor and positioned the wooden blocks before bringing the explosive device out of the hangar through the double doors. Naomi had started taking photographs of the inside of the hangar showing the racks of bombs with one or two close ups of serial numbers and pictures of the uniformed guys showing insignia of USAF. She also found some paperwork in the office with RAF Alconbury on the top and lists of serial numbers beneath which we borrowed!

I drove the Renault, its additional load out of the base back to the café car park and Naomi followed with the jeep plus its occupants. We left them in the back of the car park in a dark corner and departed the MacDonald's site as quickly as we dared with our precious cargo. We had moved the troopers because they would cause more searching for before they started looking for us. I was mulling over in my mind what they had seen. They hadn't seen me at all; they had seen a disguised Naomi, but more significantly they had seen the car with a trailer. The number plates were false as they always are when I use my vehicles on an operation but the horse trailer may be more easily identified.

"It's just after three Naomi," I said thinking out loud.

"Yes Patrick!" she replied, "Why are you behaving like a speaking clock?"

"We go straight to the annexe and park the trailer in there," I went on ignoring her, "I think we will be back around 07:00 to 08:00."

"What about your staff Patrick?" Naomi asked.

"I know. They will need to be very discrete. Vince Thompson won't take any notice but Bill and Ethan are a different matter. Ethan will be overly curious and it will be keeping control of him that will be the difficulty. I need to be up front with Bill, or as up front as I am prepared to risk," I concluded. "The other question is what do we do with the bomb, long term?" I speculated, "I know what I'd like to do!"

"What is that Patrick?" she responded curiously.

"I would like to drive it to 10 Downing Street for the Government to deal with. But I think it may have to be driven to somewhere slightly less sensitive and left on the quiet. I think we have pushed our luck as far as we can go on this one!" I stated ironically.

We carried on in silence until it was time for Naomi to drive. I slept until she nudged me awake on the slip road off the M62 five minutes from home. I got out and opened the garage door and signalled for her to drive straight in. We unhitched the trailer and parked the Renault in its usual position and left the trailer near the back of the parking space. I checked the contents and it was fine so I closed and padlocked the door of the trailer and at that point Bill walked in with Vince Thompson. Vince made his way to the dojo with a muted 'Good morning'. Bill was more curious,

"Starting a stable up Patrick?"

"I've just borrowed it for a special favour Bill. It'll be here for a few days mate so keep young Ethan off it won't you please. It has to go back fairly soon," I replied briefly.

"Of course Patrick!" he said with a knowing smile.

"We have been travelling all night so heading off for a bit of shut eye!" I explained.

With that we headed back to the flat and went to bed giving Stacey instructions not to vac up this morning. When I woke there was a warm place in the bed next to me but it was not filled with the delightfully, willowy Naomi Kobayashi and was cooling rapidly. She'd gone! I must have slept very heavily because I had 't noticed a thing. What a relationship this was turning out to be. There was no nagging, plenty of energetic sex but no guarantee when we would see each other next! Oh well, I suppose that is the best either of us can expect for now. I got up and showered and went to prepare a sandwich.

"Naomi says that she'll text you!" said Stacey, smiling.

"Thanks Stacey!" I replied.

"She is a lovely girl Patrick," said Stacey, going on, "Just the sort of girl you could settle down with!"

"Hahahah," I laughed, "It is too soon to tell and I am not sure that either of us is ready to settle down," I explained.

The only reply I got was a caustic "Men!" and off she went to start patrolling the carpets with the Dyson.
I walked down to the office in the annexe; put my mobile next to the keyboard of my computer and logged on to collect messages. Yesterday was a big day for our anti-US activities with Sumisu at Menwith Hill and the BNP at Croughton. I wanted to see if there was any news. The press sites showed various photographs of the demonstrations at both of the aforementioned sites but no mention of any extraneous activity at Menwith. I was wondering what Sumisu had been up to when my phone vibrated on the workstation. It was a text from Naomi saying simply Sumisu is not replying

to his messages. I wasn't sure how to take that because he usually initiated contact, but it set me off thinking as to what could have happened? I replied that we would wait until dark and if no contact was received we would head off up to Harrogate and see what could be found out there. Naomi said that she would meet me in the town itself by the station at 19:00.

I never get to see her car. Not that it is important but I am curious as to the style. I reckon an MG or an E-Type Jag, something to suit her long legs! She was carrying a small bag and dressed in black when I spotted her in the doorway of the station. I tried to sneak up on her but she spoke as I approached,

"Evening Patrick," she said smiling coyly.

I kissed her cheek in reply and took her hand, leading her off to the Jag. Again I was dressed in dark clothes – but smart hence the smart car. Harrogate is a very high-class area and my top vehicle would not look out of place. Before we set off to Menwith Hill we needed to have a strategy of some description.

"Have you heard anything?" I asked. Naomi just shook her head in response. "I've been on the Internet and there is no sign of any unusual activity."

"It may be that we need to stop using our mobiles Patrick. The signals are traceable," she responded.

"Maybe that's the reason he has not been in contact. Perhaps his battery is dead or the phone is broken, it could be nothing more serious than that," I speculated.

She didn't even validate my statement with a reply! She was worried however, I could tell by the stillness in her demeanour. It is the Aikido training, the psychological preparedness that she was working towards in case of the need for action. We drove on in silence until we were about five minutes away from the base where I pulled over in a convenient farm gate.

"We will stroll on the lane and see what we can see. Have you got your camera?" I asked.

"Yes Patrick," she said.

We set off along the road hand in hand chatting and heading towards a pub that is situated 200 yards passed the main entrance to the RAF Menwith Hill. There was little to see apart from a guardhouse next to a gate that consisted of nothing more than a bar across the entrance road. Well at least on the face of it that was all we could see, until I noticed something.

"Don't make it obvious Naomi but do you see smoke rising above the far buildings?" I whispered in her ear.

She responded by taking out her camera and snapping a series of photographs and slipping it back in her bag. The movement was as rapid and economical as to be scarcely noticeable and she didn't break step either. What a mover! We

continued our walk and arrived at the pub shortly afterwards. We did what was expected and bought drinks, sat down and chatted while listening to the conversations round us.
Thursday night and it was quite busy. There were a number of American accents and they weren't quiet! Made overhearing very easy!

The gist of the conversations was round the fact that the regular demonstration that usually occurs on a Tuesday had two goes this week; and,
'How the hell did the bastards get in to the facility and start a fire before they were caught?' complained one guy. 'Yeah but we got them in the end!' stated another.

Naomi and I looked at each other pointedly.

"Yep they will be in court tomorrow but then they'll let them go!" complained another.

We finished our drinks and headed back to the car, returned to Harrogate, booked an overnight hotel and enjoyed a few hours relaxation. The following morning we were up bright and early and at the courtrooms for nine. The group were on the list for first case. We took seats in the public gallery. The charge was disturbing the peace and criminal damage. The miscreants were led in en masse but that was where we were stunned. There was no sign of Sumisu! 'Shit – where is he?' I thought.

"Sometimes it is enough to load the bullets into a gun and allow someone else to fire it!" came the whisper from behind and between us.

We turned as one to see the retreating back of our mentor. We rose quietly and followed. He waited at the door and we strolled out to the famous Betty's Tearooms for early morning coffee and an explanation.

"I believe our little activities are beginning to bear fruit. You need to get rid of your mobiles Naomi and Patrick, or at least the sim cards," he began. "I had a communication from our centre regarding some tracking that has been going on and it would make sense to have an instrument that you only use for 'work' and a personal phone also but with a different number and service provider," he concluded.

"Sumisu I understand you set up the guys in the dock but why get us up here?" I enquired.

The reply was as enigmatic as it was succinct,

"I needed a lift!"

We all three laughed and enjoyed the rest of our break, apart from the bill! Betty's is world famous throughout Yorkshire (!) and charges appropriately! We headed off back to my place.

Chapter 11

The next few days were spent in collecting information from the BNP and UKIP and also sending on sensitive photographs of the cluster bomb and evidence of its previous storage facility. That thing was still residing in my annexe! We also sent copies of the evidence to the Government, national dailies and Green Peace! The reactions were really hotting up now and there had been student demonstrations, you could always rely on the students! The politicians are panicking and making statements about the strength of the 'special relationship' between our two countries, while trying to minimise the impact on the people of the US.

UKIP had produced a very attractive and well-designed leaflet outlining a change in their foreign policy, including a new section on the relationship between the USA and us. They had also included in the 'blurb' the amount of land ceded to the US under the heading of RAF airbases. As yet I had failed to convince them of the value of a strengthened relationship with France and Germany. That needed more work.

The BNP I am more concerned about because they have continued looking for areas where they can cause problems. It looks like I may have unleashed a tiger! I hope that it doesn't come to a position where I have to stop them, that could be much more difficult.

What we needed to do now, that is Sumisu, Naomi and I was to create the next part of the process of divorcing ourselves from the West and firming up the connections with our European neighbours. To that end the pair of them were coming to meet with me in a couple of days' time. I already had the germ of an idea for the cluster munitions!

Sumisu was the first to arrive, a week after we had picked him up in Harrogate. He was obviously in good spirits and seemed to be bursting with energy as a result, unusually so for this normally calm and controlled elderly gentleman. Naomi arrived a couple of hours later in her normal manner, calm and relaxed, but she too was smiling.

"Hi Patrick," she said when she walked in.

We exchanged pleasantries and discussed what had gone before including the growing furore around the keeping of cluster bombs on British territory. The Americans were embarrassed but belligerent as they would be, always believing that they were right and it's everyone else that is in the wrong.

"Well Patrick," continued Sumisu, "What have you planned to do next?"

I paused for thought and reflected on my idea for the bomb but started with,

"UKIP must keep the pressure on the government and announce their change in Foreign policy to begin with. They seem happy to continue with that as long as I feed them money! BNP do not need any further encouragement. Certain of their membership may be hard to keep tabs on! I'm not giving them anymore specific engagements but will be watching the situation carefully. As for us I've had the germ of an idea that would bring a deal of discredit to one of the main political parties if successful," I paused for effect.

"Come on Patrick!" instructed Naomi with a playful tap round the back of my head.

"Ok, ok!" I went on, "We take the cluster bomb and dump it on a notable MP's front door step!"

I waited for a reaction. Sumisu nodded sagely and Naomi smiled.

"There is only one problem that I can foresee," started Naomi, "We are short of a forklift to take the bomb from the trailer."

"Also," added Sumisu, "Leaving a bomb in a public place is ill-advised and could turn the tide of publicity against us."

"Everything you say is the truth my friends. However, I'd thought that the bomb could stay in the trailer. With regards to its safety that is a risk but I believe if we surrounded the bomb with bales of straw and ensure that the MP concerned knows where it is as soon as we have it positioned, along with the press of course, I'm 99% sure we will achieve our aims without endangering the public," I concluded. "I also believe I can find the ideal place for the bomb in the MP's constituency!"

"It sounds to me Patrick that you have already had some ideas with regards to where you will site this weapon." commented Sumisu.

"Yes come on Patrick, tell all!" egged Naomi.

"The constituency in question is South Shields on the north east coast," I went on, "There are considerable stretches of bare coastline, which at this time of year, December, are relatively deserted. Just beyond the main promenade is a track down to a beach that is almost surrounded by water even at low tide but is never quite covered when the tide is high. What I am proposing is we drive the trailer down to the beach and put it on this slightly raised area and then cordon it off. We then contact the MP and the local media and tell them where it is then sit back and watch the fun!" I finished with a smile.

"Well Patrick, your plan seems erm…. watertight!" quipped Sumisu at which we all laughed.

      I contacted UKIP and BNP, congratulated them on their good work cautioning the latter not to get too enthusiastic but without eliciting any guarantees from their bogus rep. I can see that I may have to 'discourage' him at some point. UKIP's Jason Smith was as happy as the proverbially pig in muck. They were getting more publicity than they could have dreamed of and so much more political support. I spent a couple of days collecting some necessary equipment that I stored in the trailer and by Friday evening we were ready to go. I checked the tide times and it would be low at 07:15 and again twelve hours later, so we had a choice. Common sense would say that it needed not to be left over a high tide at night in case it was stormy so we could aim for tomorrow morning or maybe Sunday. I decided that there was no time like the present so I shared this with my confederates and we decided we would leave at 04:00. We would be working in the dark, cold and wet, whichever time we chose so we included torches and waterproofs in the equipment. We turned in early, Sumisu in the annexe, and Naomi and I in the apartment, and arranged to meet him down there at 03:15

    It was a cold clear night. If the vehicles had been parked outside we would have been clearing frost away before we could set off. Thank goodness for the annexe, it also allowed us to hitch up the trailer indoors, so by the time that was done we were still warm and the Renault's engine had warmed up, as had the Mercedes SLK. We had decided that two vehicles might be necessary with three of us going, so Naomi would drive the Merc while I drove the bigger vehicle. It was a journey of only a couple of hours so there was no need to change driver and it was not necessary to rush. Rather than draw attention to ourselves we stuck to the speed limit and had a trouble free journey north.

    Once we arrived in South Shields we rumbled up the inappropriately named Beach Walk, which is as wide as a three-lane road, and found the track towards the sea at the end of the tarmac that I had spotted on Google Earth. It is a narrow track and in the dark I slowed to a crawl and also turned my headlights off travelling with just sides. I eased my way along the track for about 100yds and then stopped and got out. I found my torch, and along with Naomi, scouted ahead. All seemed to be quiet apart from the waves rhythmically rolling up the beach and then receding with a sound akin to a hiss as the sand was disturbed by the water. There was no wind and it was dry but very cold as it often is on the coast.

    We started to descend towards the beach and there was a bit of an apron before the shallow channel that surrounded the raised part of the beach that tended to remain dry. We decided to turn the vehicle on that apron and reverse on to the sandy hillock from there. Back to the Merc and on to the apron leaving the Renault a little way back on the track. There wasn't much room to manoeuvre and I started to circle as wide as I dared to the left and then back on myself. It was like towing an elephant. As soon as we hit less firm sand I had to keep going or else the trailer would have stuck in the soft material. I managed to turn so that the Renault was facing back the way we had come. I started to edge backwards but it was like driving the trailer down into the sand. The first snag that we had hit!

Fortunately I had realised that we may struggle and so some of the extras I had acquired (!) were half a dozen metal mesh barriers that I had found kicking around outside a local football ground originally intended for crowd control. I had taken them for two reasons, the main one being to throw a barrier round the trailer so that no one would get hurt, but as a way of getting across soft sand I have to admit it was rather serendipitous. We got four of them out and put them in line behind the trailers wheels. I tried again and this time the trailer rode on them and up on to the sandy knoll. We retrieved the barriers and positioned them between the trailer and the land along with some traffic bollards that I had purloined. I then started to take out other items from the trailer and both Naomi and Sumisu looked astonished.

"Patrick, what are you doing?" asked Naomi trying hard not to laugh.

What I had was an American flag and signs with skull and crossbones, along with **Danger Keep Away** boards, which then I used to decorate the trailer, barriers and bollards. The final sign that almost covered the upper half of one side of the trailer simply said '**The Property of your local MP**'

By this time they were both laughing out loud. Naomi took out her camera and started taking photographs.

"Okay let's retreat to a safe distance and see what happens," I ordered.

I took out my phone and rang a contact number for our target MP and the local press, and finally ITV and the BBC. The last call I made was to the nearby police station and explained that there was a bomb on the beach and gave them the location.

"I think we will have an hour before we get a response!" I stated.

"Yes Patrick, let's hope it is not too long. It is not warm," replied Sumisu.

Naomi just grabbed my arm and snuggled in close.

"We should go back to the main road and observe from there," I said.

We were less than 100yds from the beach but we could park up in the dawn light and observe the activity. As we were higher than sea level and all congregated in the seven seated Renault we had a good view. We waited what seemed an age but it was only just over half an hour before there was any sign of activity. A lone police officer arrived in a patrol car and walked down to the beach. He paused for a few seconds, I could imagine his thought processes galvanising into action, and then he took out his radio and obviously called for assistance. From then on the intensity of activity increased. More cars arrived, what looked like a bomb disposal team, and cameras flashed.

"Our work is done Patrick, I think we should go." said Sumisu.

We got into our cars and set off down the coast road to the south in the improving light of the dawn.
    It should have been a trouble free journey but we hadn't been going for much more than 10 miles when I noticed headlights in my mirror staying a fixed distance behind me! Naomi was driving the Mercedes and leading me. I speeded up and the guy behind me speeded up but got no closer. I slowed down and so did he. I was in no doubt that we had a tail. I flashed my lights 3 times slowly at Naomi and Sumisu. That was our prearranged signal for this very instance. Naomi slowed and I overtook her, as did my unwanted follower then I speeded up to the national motorway speed limit. The car behind, even in the gathering light of the day looked just like an ominous dark shape.
    My mobile phone informed me that I had received a text. '**Black Volvo estate – 2 occupants**' Now I knew what we may be dealing with. I put into action the next part of our plan for this situation and pulled into a Little Chef. I left my car and went straight into the restaurant and ordered breakfast and coffee. Whether I got the chance to eat it would be another matter!

While I waited I pondered which organisation our two erstwhile followers represented. Were they Police, CIA or Secret Services? All three were a possibility and they were being very careful. I was looking out for two people to come into the restaurant after me but only one arrived. I had picked up a newspaper and was 'hiding' behind it when a tall, well-built, serious looking man came in scanned the restaurant before proceeding to the bathroom. He was wearing a black wool coat, a trilby hat, and black, highly polished shoes. I had to make a decision. The other guy also had to be got away from the car. I took the step of following the first man into the toilets with a view to holding him there until his mate came looking for him. He was washing his hands and looking in the mirror. I made to walk passed him to the cubicles and he was obviously expecting something as his hands became still. I didn't disappoint him but I did surprise him. Keeping my upper body normal I hit him above the knee with the heel of my foot, a move guaranteed to ruin the ligaments and cartilages in his knee and disable him because of the pain and damage. He cursed bitterly but briefly as I hit him between the eyes with the heel of my palm rendering him unconscious. I grabbed him under the armpits took him on to a cubicle and sat him on the toilet. I tied his hands behind him and round behind the plumbing with the belt from his trousers and gagged him with his handkerchief. He wouldn't be moving for quite a while. I checked his pockets for ID and found a CIA card in his jacket, which was one question answered. I returned to the café and my breakfast had arrived. I looked round and there was no sign of anyone else. I knew that Sumisu and Naomi would wait until there was some movement from the injured guy's partner before they sabotaged the car, which was the action that we had planned in the event of such a problem arising. I played with the food on the plate as it cooled and congealed, watching the door all of the time.

A small man similarly dressed as the guy in the toilets and around 5' 7" entered the restaurant looking extremely disturbed. He marched straight across to me and hissed,

"Where is my partner?"

"I'm sorry. Do I know you?" I replied calmly.

"Don't come that with me Mister!" he snapped.

"I think you must have a problem sir - waiter!" I called.

"Shut up!" he ordered.

Too late the young lad waiting tables was hurrying across to respond to my call.

"Can I help sir?" he stammered looking terrified.

The tension between us was palpable.

"Get lost kid!" chummy bossed.

"I think this gentleman is disturbed. Can you call…." I didn't get any further.

Uttering an expletive under his breath he stormed off towards the toilets at which point I shoved a £20 note into the waiter's hand and headed for the door. Once outside I ran to Sumisu's car and told them to get out of there before going to the big Renault and accelerating out of the car park. There was no sign of pursuit but I felt sure that there would be eventually. If I was in their shoes I would scream foul long and hard at the police and give the details of the vehicle I'd been pursuing. I needed to contact Sumisu. I used my mobile with the hands free kit and once I had spoken to them I explained what I thought would happen and decided that they should remove the false plates, and Naomi should ride with me in the Renault and Sumisu drive the Mercedes SLK. If we were caught then the change in personnel and plates should cover us. It may be necessary to change these two vehicles sooner than originally planned but if necessary I would. In fact, thinking about it, I probably had no choice!

We met up at the next lay-by and I suggested Sumisu leaves the A1 and transfers to the A19 heading south. After a brief conversation Sumisu took the next turn off east and Naomi and I west towards Boroughbridge and south through Ripon and Harrogate avoiding motorways. With a bit of luck they will not find us again on this journey.

That was how it turned out. We got back to the Annexe in the late afternoon after our detours to find that Sumisu was waiting for us. First job was to get rid of these vehicles but it would have to wait until tomorrow. We decided to go and relax in the apartment and discuss the ramifications of what had happened so far.

Stacey, Bill and Ethan were in the two flats when we arrived up there. Stacey volunteered to cook us all a meal. Bill and Ethan had started on the changes in the new section and it was decided they would join us once they had cleaned up. After showers and a change of clothes we were all sat round the table enjoying the pan of chilli and rice that Stacey had cooked up. I looked round and, feeling quite detached, observed the 'family' that we had all become part of now. I was pondering the idea that Stacey, Bill and yes, even Ethan, had a right to know what they were involved with. The downside was the risk, the more people that know what I really get up to the greater the chance of discovery.

Sumisu must have been watching me because as we approached the end of the meal he suddenly said,

"Patrick, shall we go out and walk for a few minutes!" with a smile.

We stood and left the flat and walked side by side up the hill and slowly,

"You are thinking about telling your staff about the work that we do," he stated. It wasn't a question! "Naomi and I are not part of your organisation; rather you are part of ours! That is not to say that they should not be told of some of the things in which we are involved. If you do not mind my thoughts on this,"

I shook my head.

"Can I suggest that you tell them that as well as accountancy we also work on injustice in the world outside the normal realms of the law because we can get things done more quickly? I would advise against giving any information on methods we use or the name of the organisation that we represent. This would not preclude giving small but significant tasks to our friends," he concluded.

"I appreciate your input Sumisu san and agree totally with what you've said. By allowing them into our confidence we can also prepare them in the event of visitors like the CIA," I responded.

"Yes. That was a problem. I wasn't sure that they knew who we were because they'd have been here before now. If the authorities had known of you when you were in the US they would never have let you leave. This leads me to the conclusion that there is some kind of tracking device on the cluster bomb itself. What I would also do is check the vehicles and your property for listening devices. That is the only other way they can have found us, but I think that unlikely," he finished his little monologue with a smile and a bow, and a,

"Shall we return to our friends?"

We strolled back to the flat and along with coffee and brandy we sat everyone down in the lounge and told them about our 'work'. It was taken quite well, with few unsurprising questions; I felt more would come later when everyone'd had time to think. Ethan's eyes were like chapel hat pegs. He obviously didn't expect us to be working outside the law at times. What he didn't know and probably never would was that his mentor, yours truly, had committed murder in the name of justice on several occasions. Some people should not be allowed to breathe the same air as the rest of us! I glanced at Bill who was looking very thoughtful. He's the only one familiar with my weapons and I wondered how much he had guessed. I hoped it didn't cause the breakdown of our association because it has taken a deal of time to train him, his wife and now his nephew up to the level that is useful to me.

The following day I took the Renault to a local car showroom and arranged to exchange it for the Megane with all the trimmings. A couple of days later I changed the Mercedes for the M Class Grand Edition with the ML 300 CDI BlueEfficiency engine and had a tow bar fitted costing over £150k! It was nearly three times faster than the Renault! I also acquired a new set of false plates. I asked Bill to sort out the inside of the Renault Megane so that I could carry my weapons and also, to make room for the sniper rifle in the new Mercedes.

Chapter 12

We met together a few days later after having had a break that was intended to cool the situation and for Sumisu to use his contacts to ascertain the role of the CIA in what had happened on leaving South Shields. We were still unsure as to how they got on to us and now why they haven't followed up. True we had changed vehicles but the personnel were the same and none of us are exactly hidden. Sumisu came with little extra information apart from the fact that the agents were based in the UK! I am not shocked by that just a little disappointed. Perhaps that is why there has been no further action from them, when all said and done they are not supposed to be here!

We needed to review what has happened as a result of our activities. The cluster bomb was a major coup. It had created a media storm the like of which we could not have imagined. The sitting MP in the affected constituency has been forced to resign; even some of the mud has stuck to his brother, the man hotly tipped to be our next Prime Minister. The USA media are up in arms also although I can hardly see why! They were affronted that someone should go on to 'their' land and steal one of their munitions conveniently forgetting that they are in someone else's country complaining about a weapon that is illegal.

There is a growing storm gathering and orchestrated by the media moguls and their staff. I think it is time to invite the German and French secret service to the party.

I put that point over to Sumisu and Naomi and they did not disagree. Sumisu did ask the most pertinent question,

"What do you want them to do exactly Patrick?"

In all honesty I was at a loss to begin with but it came to me that we wanted their support in driving the US out of Europe so that we can maintain our independence. So we need the French and German Secret Service to find similar problems in their own countries and exorcise them. Our role is simply to tell them where to look based on our experience. The other factor is do they have any information about the whereabouts of CIA in the UK. The incident in the northeast was disturbing to say the least. Where did they come from and where are they now, can the Europeans help with that?

Sumisu would go off to France and Naomi to Germany for answers to these questions. I needed to contact the police and ask them for the owner of a certain motor vehicle, namely the one that Naomi had disabled in the Little Chef up the A1.

Initially I rang the Little Chef and spoke to someone who had been on duty the day of the 'incident'. He was full of it! They had to call an ambulance. A Yankee had been beaten up in the toilets. His mate disappeared. Then the good news, the car was still in the car park! I asked him for the registration number of the car and the make and year and if it is a hire car from Avis. The lad came back with everything I needed. That saved me a trip. All that was required now was to find out from which office the car was rented and by whom. I started ringing round the different offices of Avis and requesting the necessary. I began with the English offices, which turned out to be a mistake. The only instance of an American hiring a car recently was in Glasgow and they confirmed that the number plate I gave was one of theirs although they pointed out that cars do move around. I asked them to confirm when it was last hired out from their office and they said that it was for a week and that turned out to be the week we left the cluster bomb in South Shields. Now I had to ask the crunch question,

"Did the gentleman give a name and address?" I asked quietly.

The response was to be expected I suppose,

"Who are you?" he asked.

"Detective Inspector Pete Drysdale of the Northumbria Police Force," I came back quickly.

"Oh ok! Well I don't suppose it will do any harm!" he went on, "Mr D Brown was the name given but the address is just Bells Hill, Glasgow. That is a big area Inspector."

"Yes I am aware of the area, thank you for your help. I may have to come and look at your paperwork" I concluded the call.

Very inconclusive! Looks like I will have to go to Glasgow after all. I told Naomi and Sumisu and they said that it sounded like a good idea to identify the place where the CIA are operating from so that we can stop that but it would be useful also to find contact information to other offices in Europe. On the other hand how likely is it that the address given is legitimate? The only factor that is convincing me that it could be a genuine address is that they have to provide realistic enough ID to be able to hire a car. Offices have computer equipment that will identify if an address is correct in a matter of seconds. True the CIA will have high class forging facilities but that address must exist, it has to be checkable!

The next day armed with my policeman looking coat and a 'warrant card' as well as my Satnav I set off in the new Merc to 'run it in' with a long trip to Glasgow. I left early, planning to be in the Avis office by lunchtime, allowing three and a half hours to complete the journey. Once in the office I flashed my warrant card at the girl behind the desk and she ushered me into an inner office. I was joined by a lad of about 25 years of age who described himself as the 'manager'! I told him what I wanted and he produced a file for the week in question and the car that had been hired out. He started to read the information. I held out my hand and waited for him to hand over the paperwork with a quizzical expression. He handed the file over rather reluctantly. When I looked at the paperwork it was indeed signed by a D. Brown and the address given is in Bells Hill. I wrote down the postcode and the house number thanked the young man and left. I entered the details into my Satnav and set off to Bells Hill, a distance of about 10 miles. Once I got to the street I pulled up at the end and parked. The street was quite long and not in the best part of town, consisting of a number of brick built terraced houses some occupied and some boarded up. The one I was looking for came into the latter category. Now that I found strange because they normally put up a more acceptable front than nipping in and out of a disused property which would arouse suspicion.

I decided to stick around and watch what happened. It was cold sat in the car and as the day wore on it grew colder and, unusually, totally unprepared for a long wait. I'd not thought this one through, but Glasgow in December can be pretty damn cold so I waited until dark and then got out of my car to get my circulation going again. The house was in a set of three that were all boarded up. I was on the opposite side of the street but could see lights flickering between the boards and round the edges of the door and adjacent window. Returning to the car I took out the special toolkit held in the boot. I should have come in the Renault, this Merc was far too conspicuous and I'll be lucky to have four wheels left when I return to it! This trip had not been well planned. I'd informed Sumisu - but to just come haring up here! So I had discovered the whereabouts of a couple of operational CIA people. Now what? Shoot them? Ask them what they think they are doing operating in the UK? Jesus what a nerd I can be at times!

    I sent a message to Sumisu and Naomi explaining where I was and what I have found. Then I strolled round the block and back to the car just in time to see a couple of likely lads eyeing it up like cat's eyeing up a plate of fish. I got in and drove it to the local rail station car park, which was considerably safer. I went into the building but calling it a station is flattering. It is no more than a glorified bus shelter with a drinks and snacks machine. I bought a 'coffee' and took it back to the car where I sat and tried to drink it and think. It was like sand in suspension contained in superheated water!

    We needed to find their contacts and spread the news. There was no need to harm them physically, but photographs in the press and on TV as well as locations would have the desired effect on all governments involved including the Scottish Assembly.

I received a message back from Naomi saying be careful, find a hotel, see you tomorrow. Succinct as usual! I used my Samsung to Google 'Bells Hill – Hotels'- and found The Redstones Hotel on the northern edge of the area. A newly refurbished four-star hotel with a very comfortable bar that I got myself ensconced in for the evening. I sent texts of the location and sat down to think myself back in control. After dinner I walked briefly to aid digestion and then turned in for the night.

Naomi joined me at breakfast. She had come to listen to my plans and help carry them out if feasible! Thankfully, because of the time I have had to think in the last few hours, it has given me the opportunity to firm up my ideas. In many respects, if the plans work, then the differences between the USA and UK will be huge and irreversible. All I need to do is provide the proof of inappropriate actions by the CIA in the UK. Easy to say!

"It sounds very feasible Patrick. All we need to do then is get into their 'safe house' steal and photograph evidence, escape without being discovered and then 'publish' our discoveries?" Naomi stated sarcastically.

"I know what you mean!" I replied rather lamely. "What I suggest is going to have a look at the house tonight and see if we can spot people and patterns of behaviour."

"Sounds like a reasonable start Patrick. Have you any idea how many people are inside?" she asked in a more business-like tone.

"In all honesty Naomi I don't really know what we have in the house I've looked at. It could be a set of squatters!!" I replied defensively.

"Then you are quite correct Patrick. We need to do some observing and the sooner the better!" Naomi concluded.

That statement shaped how the rest of the day and most of the night would develop. We dressed casually and called for a taxi. There was no way I was taking the Merc anywhere near the Bells Hill property! I asked the taxi driver to drop us on the corner of the road and we put up umbrellas because it was falling damp and strolled towards our target. The weather had turned 'Scottish' that is misty, damp and bitterly cold making the air temperature that was recorded at 3 degrees Celsius feel about ten below! The drab, dull red, brick frontages of the terrace did nothing to alleviate the depressing nature of the road. It was such a dull day the streetlights had never switched off and they seemed to add to the depression by colouring everything with a sickly, yellow glow. The gardens varied from neat and tidy to dumps for old prams, bikes, soiled mattresses and various other discarded toys and household equipment. Our target property was in the latter category and in the excuse for daylight we have at the moment the shutters covering windows and doors of all three empty houses were made of sheets of metal bolted to the surrounding brickwork. They were the only aspect of the property that looked new and fit for purpose.

We continued walking to the end of the street before turning the corner and crossing the road to a bench overlooking an adjacent park.

"Did you notice anything about the house?" I asked Naomi.

"There were three together, unoccupied and the windows and doors were boarded up, however, I did think that there was something different about the middle door Patrick. The other houses had their screens bolted outside the doorframe on to the bricks but the middle door was covered but the frame was visible. It would be possible to open the middle door!" she concluded.

"Yes that is what I noticed too, and also the garden is more flattened in front of that door," I stated. "Maybe we should have a look round the back as well. This type of house has a short yard and a gate leading to a single-track road that allows for rubbish collections. It may be our way in to the property when we do need to get in," I finished.

Naomi collapsed her umbrella and stored it in the copious bag she carried with her. She snuggled closer under my defence against the weather linking arms and said,

"We can't watch the house very well from here Patrick!"

"And I thought you were getting friendly!" I retorted

After she had slapped me playfully, she stood up dragging me with her and we strolled, arm in arm, towards the back street at the rear of the house we'd targeted. It was typical of pre-war architecture, a narrow cobbled road, glistening yellow in the sickly light of the day. Head high gates set in slightly higher brick walls led into small yards full of the clutter and detritus of modern day life. Some of the more optimistic tenants had taken down the walls and tried to introduce plants into the otherwise brick and concrete yards but the poor specimens looked as drab and disinterested in life as their owners. One or two houses had flattened the lot and used the levelled area to park a vehicle some of which were rusting slowly in position, looking as if they hadn't moved in millennia!

Not so our targets! The rears of the properties were as originally intended and the gates looked remarkably well preserved in comparison with some of their neighbours. There was something at the back of my mind causing me to think of the three properties as a single unit. It was not beyond the bounds of possibility that they are using all three!

I pulled the collar of my coat higher up round my ears and neck and suggested in a whisper to Naomi that she covered her nose and mouth with the scarf she was wearing. Blessed with afterthought Steele! The idea of them using all three houses had led me to thinking that if this was an important property for the CIA then they will have cameras! Not the usually visible sort but something much more clandestine. I know that is what I would do.

We paused for a surreptitious snog on the opposite side of the street so that I was facing the back of the CIA house and Naomi had her back to it. We moved on, walking even more slowly but spotted nothing more of interest, planning to share our findings later. When we did I told her of my thoughts regarding the three houses, cameras and the possibility of this being an important facility for the CIA. Overall my Asian buddy agreed but typically pointed out something that I'd missed and that was the skylight bedroom windows that were not boarded up and that there was an empty property in the street opposite and just a little higher up. We could possibly use that property as a base for ourselves.

We continued on until we found a café near the railway station that served large pots of incredibly strong steaming hot tea, which we both drank with a grimace at the amount of tannin but loving the heat the liquid restored into our frozen and damp bodies. The outcome of our half hour break was that we would investigate the empty property in the next street to the CIA and see if we could use it to spy on the spies! To that end we set off to view the property from the front which we found offered no usable entrance so went returned to the rear. We approached from the top end of the back street so that we were not passing their house again, and were very quiet taking every precaution. Not only did we not want the CIA to spot us but none of the neighbours either. The last thing we require is someone ringing the police!

Once inside the yard, the gate was not locked, I guessed that the council had seen it was so rotten that there was no point in trying to make it secure, we were confronted by the steel covers over doors and windows. They were very sturdy and even with the help of my Swiss army knife it was a titanic struggle to free enough of the bolts to ease beneath and unpick the lock on the door. Thank goodness for the weather, there wasn't anyone about! Finally, after a good half hour, we were in! Using hooded torches we started exploring. The downstairs had two good-sized rooms; one had been a kitchen, large enough to accommodate a table, opening into the yard, then a long a passageway on the left was another door leading to the lounge. There was a cupboard under the stairs a bit like Harry Potter's first bedroom at the Dursleys'. Up the first flight of stairs there were two bedrooms of about equal size and a family bathroom. There was another staircase leading to the attic bedroom with a skylight window at either end. The general condition of the inside of the house was dry and very cold with signs of dampness encroaching into the rooms from above and below.

The torches were superfluous in the attic bedroom as the murky daylight was enough to work with. The window at the rear allowed a reasonable view of the CIA house, enough to facilitate the observation of anyone entering or leaving the back of their property. Naomi had binoculars and we also had a flask of coffee, I couldn't stand any more tea, and sandwiches to keep us going. We settled down to observe, taking half hourly spells as it was a standing roll and quite draughty by the window. All was very quiet. There was little noise from the occupied houses either side of us, just the occasional bang of a door. It remained like this until late into the afternoon when the sky had darkened and the mist developed into a continuous, soaking, heavy drizzle.

Headlights turned into the bottom of the street, the end that we had approached initially many hours ago. The vehicle was some kind of parcel van, painted a dark brown, without any markings on the sides. Everything happened very quickly. The van pulled up, two people got out on the far side and went into the yard of the CIA house and then were gone, and the van was also gone in a flash.

In that brief instant so much had happened, very little of which was observable. I stared at all aspects of the CIA house but caught nothing else. As the evening wore on we got colder and apart from the odd glimmer of light, saw nothing more. I tried the infrared sniper sight that I had brought out from a pocket buried deep in the recesses of my Gortex jacket, but with no greater benefit.

After another four hours, taking us to just after 22:00, we were beginning to think of giving up when our van arrived again. I left Naomi observing while I sprinted downstairs and got close enough to read the van number plate. The driver got out of the van and went round to the far side to help someone get out of the vehicle. There were two pairs of legs supporting a hobbling man in between them.

If my calculations are correct, including the van driver, that would be five people I'd observed. That is some deployment of resources in terms of manpower and probably equipment! The van left with the driver plus one who had got back in, and I went back upstairs to Naomi. We decided to leave at that point and return to the hotel resolving to come back the following day.

On the way back to the hotel we asked the taxi driver to find us a take away, which turned out to be Chinese, before returning to Redstones. We received a disapproving look from the Night Porter but proceeded, laughing, to our room. All an act for the benefit of any observers! Once inside we showered to re-establish some semblance of circulation in our extremities, got into bed together and ate our food side by side. We sent messages to Sumisu and asked him to check the property for communication links as well as telling him about the van, its number plate, and the activity we had observed.

The following morning we received replies about numerous activities. UKIP were revelling in the new found publicity and support they were getting from the public and the media. The BNP were a slightly different story. They were getting too violent in their protests at Menwith Hill! The situation in the House of Commons was very interesting. The PM has had to field questions almost daily on the 'special relationship' and there had even been some anti US activity on the continent. It seemed that the can of worms was opening slowly! That would be nothing in comparison with the storm that would be created when the people learn of the CIA activities on British soil.

Sumisu had information about the CIA also. The van was registered to a Scotsman called R Burns at the Bells Hill address. How poetic! There was considerable mobile phone and satellite link activity round the property but it was impossible to say how many are working in there. I still felt that it would be no more than half a dozen. The question now was how to get in to the property and collect more information? We needed incontrovertible evidence of activity of these spies that we could publish. Their mission statement is quite open in their aims namely CIA's primary mission is to collect, analyse, evaluate, and disseminate foreign intelligence to assist the President and senior US government policymakers in making decisions relating to national security. Imagine the chaos if and when they get it wrong as had happened in the past. Hopefully we can stop them doing that again in our country. I feel that they really need their activities curtailing.

"I think we need to spend a couple of days taking photographs, following people and getting into that van and eventually the house," I said.

"Not much then Patrick!" was the smiling response.

We decided to get to the house opposite early and so set off while it was still dark. We needed the car if we were going to tail the van so that was parked at the top of the road. We had discussed a plan at length. It was fairly obvious that they would always arrive at the safe house in the same way because the opening was on the vans near side. The car would be parked at the top of the street and as soon as the van arrived we would exit our house and go to our car and wait then follow at a discrete distance. If we lost them it wouldn't be important because we can always pick it up back at the house. We would have to be very careful taking photographs and watching as well as tailing. There's no way that we could afford to be caught. We agreed that if that danger should arise we would have to take every step to escape irrespective of what measures they might be!

We set off to Bells Hill armed with cameras and weapons. The car was parked as we'd planned and we proceeded cautiously to our safe house. It was possible to get in without being observed from across the street and so we managed to regain our observation post moving quickly and stealthily. We didn't have long to wait until the van entered the street! Hurriedly exiting our hiding place we almost galloped back to the car. We were walking up the street before the van had rolled to a standstill. Once round the corner we sprinted to our car and started her up. We left the lights off and waited for what was a very few seconds before the van lurched into sight. It swung out on to our road and passed by; I did a swift U-turn and followed at a reasonable distance still without lights.

The journey was quite short. It took us to the local rail station where the two passengers left and went to catch a train. We followed the van to a different residence in the Bells Hill area where the driver pulled up on another suburban road, locked the vehicle and went into a house. I didn't hesitate. I took my lock picks and camera and went to the van. It was easy to remain unobserved on the road side because of the mass of the vehicle, and so getting in was quite straight forward. Inside the front, the two seats were bucket style and the rear of the vehicle was not partitioned off. There were an extra four seats in the back but plenty of space for storage. The van was empty. I looked for paperwork, invoices anything that would provide answers or ammunition as the case maybe but without luck. I still photographed the inside and then left the van. Naomi drove us back to the rail station where she checked on the trains that had left in the last twenty minutes. When she arrived back she said that there was only the one in to the City of Glasgow itself. Inconclusive! At this point we decided on a change of plan. We decided to follow the van and Mr R Burns. We moved the car so that it was a little further away but facing the same direction as the van as when we'd arrived. We waited. Nothing! The weather was a little kinder than the previous day in that it was dry but still drab and grey. Our boredom was relieved when Burns got back in the van but he only drove to the supermarket. Naomi followed him round and took photographs observing him while he shopped, then followed him back to the house. Nothing to report! Naomi sent photographs to Sumisu to identify properly.

    The rest of the day was spent sat in the car until Burns set off to collect people from the station and take them back to the house.

    So that is one area we have cleared up but not with a great deal of evidence. We stayed through the evening at our empty property but saw and could report nothing. Shortly after midnight we returned to the hotel. We lay in the dark, after some vigorous lovemaking to encourage the circulation to get going again, any excuse (!) and thought about our next step.

"We have to get inside the house!" I whispered.

"Yes Patrick but it is going to be risky," was her reply.

"Whichever way we attempt it there is an element of risk," I stated unnecessarily.

"We should re-assess what we know and look at ways of getting in," came Naomi's response.

"You're right of course. Okay, well we have seen the van driver who never enters the house. We have seen two lots of two men going in and one coming out then today two coming out and then going back. We know the guy that I injured is in there and has been for two days now. There always seems to be at least someone in there as a light is usually visible," I concluded.

"We need to get up to the building and ascertain what can be heard," Naomi suggested.

"I agree but we need a scanner to detect sensors and we must be on the lookout for cameras," I replied. "I'll message Sumisu and tell him what we need and in the meantime we watch their movements."

This I did and received a message back saying '*see you tomorrow - Reserve me a room*' within ten minutes. We turned over and slept until 08:30 having to rush to get up book a room for Sumisu and to make the dining room before breakfast was over.

The plan we sketched out for ourselves was to try and see signs of sensors or cameras and to record movements and identify the people using the property. It was a little brighter today and we had a clearer view of the back of the house. Using the sniper sight I scanned the tops of the walls, roof and windows but without much luck. We took a stroll round the front of the building, which seemed to be virtually unused by the spies, and proceeded very slowly taking photos with our mobile phones as we walked, then returned to our safe house to study the results.

The front of the house was almost as we thought and hardly used. The door was covered in such a way that it could be opened easily and yet seemed boarded up like all the others. An escape portal perhaps! The houses at either side were boarded up properly and so not intended as entrances or exits. The steel covered windows on the face of it offered no help either but with the assistance of the hand lens Naomi had with her, we examined the photos more thoroughly. There was the possibility of something on the doorstep but what it was we could not tell. We would have to wait until we were back at the hotel and we could print the images out and make a proper examination.

While we were studying the photographs back at the hotel we discussed the next steps.

"We must get inside!" I said again.

"Yes Patrick. Perhaps we hold up the van when it arrives, immobilise the driver plus one of the occupants and use the other to get us in," she responded.

"Yes that is probably the only way, having tried to think of other options," I commented. "I've tried to come up with alternatives and we could get some locals to assault the house or capture the inmates one at a time, but that would alert the occupants that someone was on to them. I think you could be right!" I said looking directly at Naomi. "If we can take out the driver plus two there should be only two perhaps three at the most to deal with inside. We need to do this at night, dressed in black, with Noh masks!"

"What happens if we have problems with them?" Naomi asked quite reasonably.

"We cannot be identified!" I left that statement hanging in the air for a moment. "Hopefully, we will need to do no more than injure!"

What we had just agreed was a basic level of self-protection that we always have as a minimum. Occasionally, it had been necessary! We needed to put this activity in motion as soon as possible so that we can gain maximum influence from blowing the CIA's cover. We planned to move on them tonight. To that end we had an afternoon nap and then prepared our equipment, which consisted of small arms, my Glock 17 handgun and knife and whatever Naomi carried. We didn't go in for comparing weapons; they were the tools of our trade!

It got to 20:00 and we set off to the house, which was our 'safe' house, in Bells Hill. Once ensconced we watched for the van arriving! Our plan was to get down to it as quickly as possible, immobilise the driver somehow, then take the two passengers prisoner in the van. We planned to search them for papers and ID and then use them to gain entrance into their 'safe' house. We waited! After five minutes we were getting scared! Adrenaline! We moved downstairs and eased out of the door into the yard. It was cold, but then December in Scotland tends to be! It was dry which was unusual for Scotland! Our breath plumed from frozen lips,

"We will be spotted breathing!" I gulped.

"Yes Patrick!" she responded, "We need to keep lower!"

We crouched lower! That also allowed us to keep closer to the gate and meant we were not observed from the houses at either side. We didn't have to wait much longer! The sound of an engine turned into the narrow dark back street and crept up towards us. The vehicle pulled up and we leapt into action. We'd agreed that Naomi would immobilise the driver while I held the passengers until she could come and give a hand.

She went through the small gap we had left and straight for the driver's door. I was hot footing it round the back of the vehicle and came up behind the two passengers. With the butt of my Glock I hit the one on my right at the base of his skull and then pushed the gun into the neck of his pal and forced him to the ground face down. I put my knee in the back of the second guy and waited for Naomi. She was with me in seconds secured my guy with the usual garden ties, heavy duty, and then I finished the job on the fellow that was still awake. He was trying to struggle; I put my mouth to his ear and hissed,

"Keep very still mate!" and emphasised my statement with the barrel of my Glock grinding into his neck. He kept still!

With one at either side we bundled him towards the door and I ordered him to get us inside. We had noticed that there was always a pause before they got inside when we had watched them previously. It indicated that there's some kind of password system for gaining entry. I kept my gun pressed tight into his neck until he eventually said with a snarl,

"There is a button on the right!"

I jabbed harder with the gun,

"Press it twice and then hold it in!" was his response.

"Any warning and you are dead!" I stated in a quiet whisper.

I did as he suggested and we waited. The sound of tumblers dropping and then the door began to open. I launched our captive through the door and followed him quickly. As I had hoped, the force and suddenness knocked the man inside to the floor and also grabbed the attention of another occupant who started to speak but got nowhere with Naomi going passed me like a wraith and getting behind him with her knife. I sat my captive in a chair and fastened him to it then brought the unconscious man in and fastened him to the central heating radiator that was surprisingly warm. That only left the van driver and I went out to see what the situation was there while Naomi started frisking our captives and taking photographs with the necessary ID. The driver was unconscious, well secured and gagged. I moved him to the rear of the vehicle and secured him there then started the van and drove it to the top of the road so that it wasn't blocking the back street before sprinting down to the CIA house.

Inside there were four rather angry men and one extremely calm and purposeful Asian lady taking their photographs with their ID open on their chests? The room they were in would have been the lounge, which was identical to the house opposite that we had used. There were little signs of previous occupation but indications that these men had been here quite a while. As well as the computers there was a working fridge and kettle plus fan heaters and operational central heating. I wondered who paid the gas bills! In their parlance they were in it 'for the long haul'.

Their anger was dissipating somewhat as of course they could not see what nationality we were because of the Noh masks and there is little point in anger if you have no target on which it can be vented. When they had been 'shot' with the camera we gagged them again. I recognised one of the men as the one who had the damaged knee and as Naomi started to fasten his gag he attempted to lash out at her with his head. It was then that I saw how fast she is! The Aikido skills that she had developed way beyond what I had achieved, and I'm not bad, came to the fore. As chummy tried to head butt her she moved to one side and hit him on the temple with the heel of her left hand. His head snapped back and he was out like a light!

"Let's have a look at the computers," I stated.

There were three machines and they were linked to the mains that I feared might indicate collusion with the authorities. They may have linked into the neighbours' power supply or just re-connected with the mains. We sat at the machines and tried to ascertain whether there were any accessible files that we could use. All we found were that one machine seemed to be connected to a suite of cameras that indeed covered the outside of the property but turned out to be relatively ineffectual as we'd entered with consummate ease! The other two seemed to be protected so I turned them off, disconnected them and prepared to take the base units with us. I'm sure Sumisu will have someone who can worm their way into the complexities of the hard drive. We needed to leave but it was also necessary to let someone know that these fellows were here. They would not escape without assistance. When we secured people they stayed fastened!

    I collected their mobile phones and trawled through their phonebooks for common names. I looked at the call log and saw who they had called most recently and there was one that was common to two of the phones, cryptically they had spoken to 'Bob' whoever he was! I had no intention of calling him but I did send a text the gist of which was that his boys are all tied up! Before we left we disconnected the cameras and took the base unit and a set of disks that may have had records that could be useful. We returned to our car stashed the computer equipment and went back to the safe house and once again waited. This time we had no intention of going back in but I wanted to see who came to rescue our pals!

Chapter 13

We didn't have too long to wait before two Volvo estates in charcoal grey entered the bottom of the street and approached the CIA house rather hurriedly. The first of the vehicles had four people inside and the rear one only two. They pulled up and five people exited quickly running to the door that we had entered just a relatively short time earlier. The sixth person stood outside with the cars and if I was not mistaken it was a lady! We had a camera with a night telephoto lens and were shooting away happily so that we could spend time later identifying the people and passing them on to the relevant authorities. The lady outside was making it easy; she kept turning round and giving us full face shots.

After a couple of minutes the people inside started leaving the house and getting into their cars and they hurried off.

"Well that's that for now Naomi," I exclaimed.

"Yes Patrick. It looks like we got everything that we came for," she replied. "What now?"

"Back to the hotel, a pleasant meal, bed and then back south tomorrow?" I offered.

"That sounds good. I am getting a little fed up with the cold and damp," she responded.

We left our hideout and strolled arm in arm back to the car. When we got to the top of the road the brown 'delivery' van they had used had gone also. Our plans that evening went very much as I had described apart from the fact that we forwarded copious amounts of material to Sumisu for his perusal and asked him to meet us at the Annexe in a couple of days' time.

The journey south was uneventful although I was very careful to check that we were not followed. There was that niggle at the back of my mind that in dealing with the agency we must be in danger of being found out! They were surely going to move heaven and earth once the news hit the media! We discussed this in the car and talked about the choices that were available to us. Naomi and Sumisu could disappear to wherever they go to when not with me; we could decamp to my place in France and continue from there; or we could sit tight and maintain our cover. I felt that we could do the latter for a while longer. Besides I needed to catch up with UKIP and the BNP before setting off abroad again. To all intents and purposes, with what we had collected in the last three days, we had all the evidence necessary to seriously cool relations between the UK and the USA and probably with USA and Europe also. It was our intention to pull in the DCRI and also the BND.

Naomi stayed over that night and we discussed future strategy the following morning while waiting for Sumisu. When he arrived he had some slightly disturbing news regarding BNP action.

"Patrick, the British National Party have continued their activities at Mildenhall, however they have become slightly too enthusiastic! The situation down there has become agitated and they are no longer serving the purpose for which they were engaged. In fact they could be damaging your cause! How do you think we should proceed?" asked Sumisu

I thought for a few minutes then looked at Sumisu, he liked positive responses, and stated,

"Initially I'll call a meeting with their representative and put it to him that they should back off totally until the fuss has died down. I will withdraw funding if they don't kerb the violence and if they do not follow my instructions. The one thing I will not tell them is that if they don't follow my instructions they will begin to experience injury to their personnel!" I concluded with that veiled threat.

"Sounds as though you have put some thought into that Patrick!" responded my mentor.

"When I first considered using BNP, and it was not something I did lightly, I planned my exit strategy!" I said.

"It may be that now is the time to put that into practice," he smiled.

The rest of the talk we had was around what to do with the CIA material. To begin with Sumisu and Naomi would take everything away and begin by identifying the people we'd photographed. They were then going to circulate the information to the German's and the French and send it to the Foreign Office. It was felt that we should give our own government some time to prepare a suitable response so we agreed that the media would receive the information a day later. The information would be distributed in the UK anonymously whereas the secret service departments of our European partners would receive it from me and sent to Monsieur Picard and Herr Hahn. I also suggested that Sumisu keep me up to speed with interim information where appropriate. I was particularly interested in the ID of the lady at the CIA house in Glasgow.

    My companions left a few hours later in a taxi heading for the railway station in Leeds. I spent the afternoon checking messages and mail, both paper and electronic, and catching up with my team. Ethan was doing the donkeywork in my adjoining apartment and was in fact doing a great job. The architect I'd hired had been in and suggested steps he could take and materials he needed to buy. I'd furnished Bill Fordyce with a budget that was now getting low he told me, so I arranged for him to have a couple of thousand to be going on with. I also told him that if they needed to hire any specialist tradesmen to get the best, I didn't want any old crap, however, being impatient, nor did I want to have to wait that long.

    The following day I arranged to meet with Jason Smith of UKIP and the bogus 'Smith' of the BNP, obviously not at the same time! The meeting with Jason was agreed for the following evening in the local that we had used in the past.

"Good evening Mr Smith," I began.

"Good evening Mr Steele," in a friendly enough tone.

"How are things?" I inquired.

"In all honesty Mr Steele things couldn't be better. Our membership is on the increase, the polls are very favourable to us and we are getting more column inches in the media. I must thank you for what you've done. Is it possible that you would relinquish your anonymous status so that we can thank you properly?" he asked with a wide, encouraging grin.

"There is no chance of that Mr Smith but what I do need to do is warn you that there will be no more money. I will expect UKIP to make the most of the details that will come out in the media in the next few days. You'll not be disappointed and I will contact you directly with information that will be going to the press. You have a mobile number for me if there is anything I can do for you and I will always be a friend to a party that has the welfare of the UK at heart," I concluded.

Shortly after that we finished our drinks, shook hands and went our separate ways. I just hoped the meeting with the BNP would be as easy! The message should be the same but in fact the likelihood is that I have set a rabid beast in motion and there will be no reining them in without the kind of action that they themselves understand!

That meeting was planned for the day after the UKIP at the supermarket in nearby Dewsbury. I needed to be hard on them which didn't altogether go with the laid back person that I am and the calmness instilled by the Aikido discipline. However, I will have to be like my name 'Steele' and ominous, to convince them that they cannot do as they please. One of the questions in my mind was concerning the bogus 'Smith' and his actual role at Mildenhall or has he handed responsibility over to someone else? Do they operate 'cells' as in the Gurentai? I would imagine that they do, it is the safest way to protect each other and the hierarchy of a party that is struggling to maintain a respectable side. I would have to be careful and ensure I didn't get trapped! I was fairly certain that they would be used to me arriving early and so I had it in mind to be late and see if that drew all the protagonists together. I would also have to be certain that I wasn't carrying anything that would identify me but I will be carrying my Glock knife. I could, of course, not turn up at all and just observe them, but that wouldn't work because 'Smith' had my number. I decided to be late!

The time I was supposed to be in the supermarket café was 14:00. I arrived at 14:20 and took my time. There were two missed calls on my spare mobile that I expected were from my quarry. I'd left it long enough so that his cover outside and in the store were getting twitchy and starting to move towards 'Smith'. As I arrived two of them were approaching their boss and he was giving them a right mouthful when he saw me.

"Sorry I'm late Mr Smith! Having some problems?" I asked nodding at the two departing backs.

"No! No problem Mr Steele," he hurried on, "What can I do for you?"

I spent the next five minutes concentrating very hard on my self-control and outlining the detail of what Sumisu had told me about the behaviours exhibited at Mildenhall by his group. It consisted of verbal abuse, vandalism on the edge of the base, assault in the town of US soldiers, and, fights started in local pubs near RAF Mildenhall.

He then went on quite an aggressive defensive tirade both justifying some and denying others of the accusations. His arguments were not convincing in any way shape or form.

I was beginning to experience the old red mist that I thought I had under control with the Aikido training. I adjusted my physical position took in a slow deep breath and took control once more and looked 'Smith' straight in the eyes.

"Listen very carefully to what I am about to say Mr Smith!" I stated quietly but forcefully. "The violence around Mildenhall will stop. Protesting non-violently was fine but the money stops today unless I have your guarantee that there will be no more fighting, vandalism or aggressive outbursts that will disrupt our campaign. Our public profile must remain positive!" I concluded.

I never shifted my gaze from his face. I waited for his response with an impassive expression. He was glowering back at me with the blackest look he could muster! 'Smith' stood and as he did so two of his henchman stepped into the café in as menacing way as two beetle-browed, knuckle scraping, lame brains could muster, and ambled their way towards us. I sat where I was and maintained my expression and said,

"The money stops now! I know longer want your involvement on my behalf and I thank you for what you have achieved so far," I stood, slid my chair under the table,

"Good bye Mr Smith!" I concluded and turned to the exit and walked towards the two meatheads. They were a couple of big men with tattoos and muscles and stern expressions. They stood in my way,

"Excuse me," I said.

They looked at my host who must have given them the nod and they stood aside, one of them carelessly left a foot in my way for me to trip over which I failed to do, stamping down on it instead. He went down clutching his foot and cursing by which time I'd passed the pair and was on my way. I noticed that 'Smith' was on his mobile, which I found interesting! I left in an unhurried and calm way but with my wits about me. I knew that they would be a few of them. Instead of walking to my car I proceeded on a footpath alongside the canal that would bring me out near the town centre. I could hear rapid footsteps approaching from behind, I knew who it would be and when I turned I wasn't disappointed. Here they came, four of them, one limping slightly, and 'Smith' following some distance in the rear.

I turned and faced them and relaxed myself so that my muscles were ready and not taut with lactic acid. They kept coming and as with many large, strong and confident men they were looking at my face, sneering and the front two were accelerating to the attack. I let them come on to me and as with all aspects of Aikido I used their momentum against them, as an idle bloke, it saved me energy! They threw punches at my head, which I ducked underneath and pulled their arms through kneeing one in the groin and propelling the other further away with the flat of my hand. The other two approached more cautiously and I noticed 'Smith' hesitate. I am sure he thought the first two would have me held by now and feeling sorry for myself instead of the other way round.

The second guy who I had pushed away was coming back and the other two men were approaching more cautiously. I went for the guy I'd fooled already, he was snorting like a bull! He was shocked by the speed of my approach. I hit him with the heel of my palm above his top lip and angled up against his nose. I heard the crunch, a muffled scream and fountains of blood. I turned immediately and went after the other two; crashing down on the already injured foot of the guy I'd caught inside the supermarket and striking the last one on the forehead once again with an open hand. The action felt so good because I still had that burning in the pit of my stomach that yearned for action despite the increased level of self-control that Aikido afforded me. I continued towards 'Smith', who was not looking quite as composed,

"That was very predictable Mr 'Smith' but not very clever. Now I'd appreciate it if you could take your 'pals' and go lose yourself because if I come across you again, unless it is for legitimate reasons, it will not be your thugs that are on the end of a good hiding!" I left the threat hanging in the air and strode back to the supermarket car park, to my car and drove away checking my mirror as I left.

    The following day I walked down to the annexe and after a workout, a shower and a coffee with Bill I went into the office and started pulling together the information that my confederates and I had collected. The CIA information was damning and should provide the media with a field day and the government with a headache. I contacted Sumisu and asked him if he was ready to send the information out. He confirmed that he would see me the following day.
    Sumisu arrived early with a brief case full of papers. He arrived alone, which I was disappointed about! We collected the paperwork we'd gathered together and spent almost the full day putting a portfolio of photographs and typed information into envelopes to send to various

organisations. The first set were going to Monsieur Picard in France, then Herr Hahn in Germany and finally to the Foreign Office. I sent Ethan off to the post office with the European envelopes because of the longer time it takes for post to be delivered. I am also old fashioned enough to prefer overland to internet because of the dangers of being hacked into and the attention the CIA had been attempting to afford us. The second batch we planned to send to the BBC and national dailies a day later. After that it would be a 'sit and wait' situation. When the shit hit the fan I'd hoped that the two political parties I'd engaged would fan the flames. Whatever the BNP would do was out of my hands, but I did feel that UKIP would be gleefully on board!
Now we wait!

Chapter 14

The portfolios had been in the public domain for five days before anything broke more widely. I would imagine that the sources of the information were being checked for their voracity. When things did start to emerge they began as a trickle of suggestions about the CIA and the fact that they were operating in the UK. Within another week there was more and the public in general had started to respond. I was pleased. Questions had been asked at Prime Minister's Question Time in the House of Commons. I felt this was going to run and run and would lead at the very least, to a re-negotiation of the 'special relationship' with the terms being more favourable to the UK.

I arranged to meet with Sumisu and Naomi to celebrate. I had booked a table at the George Hotel in Harrogate for 19:30. I selected the George because I had eaten there once before in a previous life! It was the first restaurant I'd eaten in where the waiter put the table napkin on your lap for you! I thought I was being assaulted! The hotel was out of the Victorian era and walking into it was like stepping back to those times. The wallpaper was red flock the tables and chairs are dark mahogany finished with pink plush. The service on the tables was heavy silver, overly ornate and the aforementioned napkins were large enough to cover a small table. The ears were not assaulted by musack but the silence was reverential to the culinary skills of the artist who masqueraded as a chef in the kitchen.

I was in the bar when Naomi arrived and Sumisu came several minutes later looking slightly less urbane than usual. In fact he seemed quite flustered.

"Good evening Sumisu san," I said with a bow. He responded in the usual way observing Japanese etiquette.

"Patrick, I have been followed!" he said quite rapidly.

I offered to buy him a brandy but he requested green tea. We retreated to a corner table so that we could observe the room while listening to Sumisu recounting to us details of his mini adventure. It seemed that from leaving the station in Leeds someone had picked him up and he'd only managed to lose him on the outskirts of Harrogate, if lose him he in fact did! These were *his* words!

"So you don't know whether or not they are aware that we are here?" I asked. Sumisu nodded and smiled slightly.

"Let us go and eat!" I said.

Sumisu and Naomi looked at each other and rose and followed me into the dining room. We were greeted and seated and supplied with menus, water and a wine list by different men who were almost invisible they were so efficient and quiet. We ordered and then returned to the subject that had so disturbed my mentor.

"Why are you so upset by this Sumisu san?" I asked quietly, remembering my Japanese manners. I have never seen the imperturbable gentleman flustered before.

"Forgive me Patrick but I feel that I may have jeopardised our unit and I have never been in this situation before. We three have grown close over the last few months. Perhaps it is time to disband and go our separate ways! I have become careless!" he concluded.

"Sumisu," I began, "It must be the CIA and with their resources we shouldn't really have been surprised. It's equally surprising that Naomi and I have not been followed. In fact we may have been, but once they knew where we were coming, backed off!" I said as steadily as the adrenalin beginning to flow in my veins would allow.

Up until this point Naomi had been gold fishing! Her mouth opening and closing with increasing rapidity!

"What are we going to do?" she hissed, "How do we get out of this mess?"

"I suggest that we eat dinner and then worry. They will try and get hold of us as we leave. We have time to think of a way around this," I postulated, "Initially my feeling is that we leave together on foot and make our way to the bus station and get on a transport of some description to anywhere but here."

We spent the time waiting for and eating the main course working out how we were to exit the hotel. The conclusion – via the kitchen or whatever rear entrance we can find. I excused myself and went to the bathroom! I scouted round the rear corridors until I found what I was looking for.

A door with a push bar that said 'Fire Exit' above it! I eased it open and took a look outside. It opened into a yard containing the sort of clutter you'd expect to find from a restaurant with a bar; boxes, beer kegs and so on. There was a double gate at the bottom that I imagined concealed a member or two of the CIA. They would leave no stone unturned.

When I returned to our table I sat quietly thinking for a minute and then told them I had found a way out. I also had a proposal to make and I didn't know how well it would go down. I suggested that I allow myself to be taken so that Naomi and Sumisu could disappear undetected. The plan was to leave via the back door and for me to attack the guys outside while Naomi and Sumisu slipped away quietly. They didn't like it but had to accept that it was the best way of some of us escaping! Also, as I said to them over coffee, the CIA operatives would have to be good!

The time came for us to move. I paid the bill and we collected our coats and prepared to leave. I led my friends to the rear of the hotel and towards the exit taking the tube out of the light in the corridor so that no tell-tale glimmer was to be seen from outside when the door was opened. I eased it open as quietly as possible and we paused to allow our eyes to become accustomed to the darkness of the night. We walked quietly down the yard to the gate, which I opened, and then strode out purposefully. There were a couple of guys either side of the gate. I turned left to walk down the back street leading away from the hotel rear entrance. The man I was walking towards stepped out and squared up, I heard footsteps coming from behind.

"What do you want?" I snapped.

The man just grinned and made to get hold of me reaching out for my arm.

"You're coming with us!" he stated in an unmistakeable southern states drawl.

He was doing the typical reach towards my upper arm and the other guy would get hold of the other side. Well that was their theory. They were both wired, the tell-tale connection leading from an ear to under the collar of their jackets. The guy approaching was on the floor before the other had got hold of my arm from behind. I'd gripped his arm pulled towards me and hit him in the upper lip/nose region with considerable force. He wouldn't be getting up. The guy approaching from the rear never got to me! Naomi had taken him from behind! We then disconnected their radios which would cause a little more delay.

"Ok Mr Lone Ranger we leave together!" she said with a smile.

We walked either side of Sumisu, who was looking quite his old self, and headed for the train and bus terminal two streets away from where we had eaten. The first transport available was a bus to Bradford, which we bought tickets for and got on without the slightest intention of going all the way. I was under no illusion that we'd gotten away Scot-free. It was my thought that once they'd come round they would be on their radios, either that or even earlier if they were supposed to check in and didn't. We sat separately on the bus, Naomi and Sumisu together like father and daughter about halfway back, and me at the front on my own. It was agreed that they would take their lead from me about where to get off. I had the idea that there would be a stop off at Yeadon about twenty minutes away and there would be other options from there. I reckoned it would be a good half hour before they got their act together and I also reasoned that Naomi was really the only one that was safe! How had they got on to Sumisu?

We arrived in Yeadon untroubled by the Americans. I allowed my companions to dismount first and waited a second or two longer before I moved. None of us knew the town particularly well and we needed to find a taxi pretty quickly. I'd concluded that providing we'd not been followed this far we could get a taxi home. The slightest doubt and we would head to Leeds instead. I allowed Naomi and Sumisu to walk arm-in-arm about fifty yards in front of me and trailed them quietly having first walked in the opposite direction and circled back round so that I was behind them on the opposite side of the street. We proceeded towards the centre of the town, which was only a couple of hundred yards away in reality. As far as I could see there was no sign of anyone following, until I noticed a saloon cruising with lights off just in front of me. It was proceeding slowly enough for me to sneak up behind and slip into the back seat. The driver, he was alone, was obviously shocked but stopped the car and stayed exactly where he was, well you would with a silenced Glock 17 thrust into your neck. I ripped the radio earpiece out and growled into his ear,

"Do not turn round or say anything!"

I was aware that he may communicate with whoever was at the other end of the transmitter. I put the earpiece in my own ear and listened, nothing.

"Turn off the engine!" I instructed.

He started to shrug but I clipped him hard with the gun and pushed it back in his neck,

"Not quick enough my friend," I said.

He pulled up as requested and I gestured for him to step out of the car. I stayed close behind him and took him round to the boot of the car, which I indicated he should open. There was no one about so when the boot, or should I say 'trunk', was opened I clipped him very hard and pushed his unconscious body inside. I searched him and removed his radio and weapon. I locked the car with the gun still inside and donned his communication equipment so I could listen in to what was going on.

I hurried after my friends and told them what had happened. I also indicated the earpiece and pantomimed that they should be quiet but we should search for a taxi. While we were waiting I phoned the police and told them about the car on the side street with a gun on the driver's seat! We got in the taxi and went straight back to my place.

All the way back I heard snatches of conversation from the CIA people but they must have realised that their man was missing and they shut down. I took the cells out of the equipment and threw the lot out of the taxi window.

It took about half an hour to get back into Dewsbury. I rang Bill Fordyce from a payphone and asked him to collect us from the railway station. We were home within a further twenty minutes and enjoying a whisky, or in Sumisu's case warmed sake! We needed something to take the edge off!

"They may have traced Sumisu san through his mobile while we were in the States and found a similar message type over here. We all need to change our sim cards again! In fact it may be wise to change the phones entirely. Use two phones, one for our domestic needs and the other for business. I don't know whether that was the way they got on to us but it is one possibility. We will get new phones tomorrow," I concluded.

The apartment next door had a bedroom kitted out so Sumisu slept there and Naomi and I in my bed. The following day we went to a local shopping centre, bought the new mobiles and found a Starbuck's for a coffee. Ironic that the only coffee shops available are American! As we moved around the newspapers' headlines were full of comment about the US and UK relationship. On TV politicians were polarising into pro and anti US groups much as they had over entering the common market in the 70s and 80s. It was good to see. The US Ambassador was backwards and forwards to Number 10 and there was speculation that the PM would visit Obama. Overall our campaign had been a success and we were achieving more than at first thought possible, but for the CIA we would be home and dry!

While we were congratulating ourselves, and at the same time worrying about maintaining anonymity, I received a text on my old phone from the BNP! All it said was *'They have taken Smith'* I replied that we should meet at the usual place at two this afternoon. I told the other two and suggested that they watch my back describing the problems I'd had in the past with the BNP. They agreed.

Chapter 15

We arrived at the supermarket in good time and I was ensconced in the café by the time two of the thugs I'd seen before came in and sat opposite me with less than welcoming and 'nice to see you' faces.

"You bastard!" started the older one, "You got him taken! You planned this! I should tear your fucking head off!"

"Good afternoon! It's nice to see you too!" I replied. "Do you think I would be here if I'd organised him being taken? I would have had no need to come! Where were you when it happened?" I asked.

"Menwith Hill, they just sent a squad of soldiers out while we were doing our usual shouting and fence rattling and they pulled their weapons and took 'Smith' inside," commented the older thug.

"Leave it with me. I will see what I can do! In the meantime any other political group would be reporting to the police that one of their members had been taken! I suggest you knock on the police station door in Harrogate and make a complaint," I finished with a smile, stood and sauntered away from them.

When we met up back at the annexe I explained to my friends what had happened and suggested that I go back up to Harrogate with Naomi and collect the Jaguar that I'd left the previous evening and while up there I may have a drive round the Menwith Hill area. What I didn't say was that I had an evil idea in mind that would cause a furore of immense proportions. I packed my sniper rifle into its hiding place in the back of the Renault and took flask, high-energy bars and a change of clothes.

"I know what you are up to Patrick!" said Naomi. "You are going to kill him aren't you?"

"Call it killing two birds with one stone!" I smiled and kissed her on the cheek.

She sighed and got into the passenger seat of the Renault and we set off to Harrogate. I gave her the spare Jaguar keys and dropped her beside the car before setting off up to the place misnamed RAF Menwith Hill. I'd used Google Earth to pinpoint where I was going because of the lack of time to prepare for the shot that I felt I was about to take. In my favour were the weather conditions, which were clear, cold and bright and expected to stay clear overnight with some frost. I'd also had to include my night sight because it was already dusk.

I picked out a place on the edge of Darley Head that is topographically higher than the Menwith facility but it gave a clear view. I was taking a chance that they wouldn't keep 'Smith' for long because of the bad publicity it would generate. I wanted to shoot him inside the compound so that he would still be in the hands of the Americans. Oh yes it was true that the man would be shot by an external source but he would be in their hands and the question was why?

I'd also brought my Glock 17 and knife partly for self-protection and as a secondary idea, which was to get into the compound and shoot or knife Smith where he was and that would be even more damning. I had to make that decision within the next ten minutes!

I parked up at Darley Head, put the sniper rifle in my 'sports bag' and strolled into the woods overlooking the camp. Calling it a camp was a bit of a misnomer. The whole facility was intended to support the radar facility and because of the peacetime situation here there was only a small fenced off area. I looked around at the edge of the woods and considered the situation. It would be very dark in about 45 minutes and a long shot would be very difficult. On the other hand stepping into the lion's den could be disastrous, but bold! I went back to the car and put the sniper rifle away. I checked my Glock and added the silencer and put my Glock knife in the ankle sheath. I changed into my black gear and ski mask! Decision made I set off back to the fenced off compound.

In my mind I'd decided to kill 'Smith' and physically there wasn't much anyone could do to stop me, but morally I was beginning to wonder whether he deserved to die. Was I going soft? I have been killing criminals and other human beings, oxygen thieves that do not deserve to breathe the same air as decent folk, for years. He was just another example of the type!

I kept to the shadows and took my time approaching the gate. There was the usual red and white barrier pole across the road and a guard in a well-lit shed – gate house – on the right as you drive up to the entrance. There was one soldier leaning on the outside smoking and I could see the head of another inside the wooden building. My problem was that I didn't want to let them know I was at the base. Only one choice then and that was to circle round and cut my way in through the surrounding chain link fence on the darkest part of the compound that I could find. I moved round behind the gate house, and on the opposite side of the road, keeping to the deepest shadows possible. I was wearing my black ski mask, shirt, jeans and trainers and as long as I followed my current pattern of behaviour I would be virtually undetectable.

I reached the point of the compound at the corner furthest away from the front entrance. There were a number of large spherical structures that constitute specialised radar used for detecting missiles aimed at the US. There was no sign of any human activity and not even many closed circuit TV cameras. I used the small aerosol of acid spray to 'open' a hole in the fence large enough for me to pass through. I entered the US base and crouched down where I was to assess the risks and my position. Everything was quiet and very dark! To my right were the radar constructions with paved walkways between that then lead to the main buildings. I stayed with the perimeter and moved forward keeping low. The base was not that big and so apart from a main block nearer the front gate there were only three other long buildings all that had some lights blazing.

I would be surprised if they were holding 'Smith' in the main block and so started in towards the rear of the nearest building that was showing the fewest lights. There were doors at either end and I eased one open slowly again staying very low. I was looking down a corridor that seemed to run the length of the building. It was empty and dimly lit. I stayed still listening intently, waited for four or five minutes, but heard nothing. I decided to move down the corridor and did so quickly on my toes carrying my now silenced Glock angled downwards and held in both hands. There were three doors down the right side and four more on the left. I paused at each listening carefully but there was no sound. The corridor was illuminated by emergency lighting only and as this was the rearmost building I suspected that it was used for storage.

    I went forward from this unit and had a look at the front one and there was altogether too much activity for me to get involved with. There were many more windows and I surmised that this may be the main accommodation block. I went back to the middle of the buildings that seemed to be designed similarly to the first that I had reconnoitred. The light emitting from round the doorframe was much brighter. I decided to try the windows to see what I could glean. They were either dark or curtained with a light behind. I listened and heard voices, a television I thought, but nothing that unusual.

    In my mind I felt that the Americans would have to hand their prisoner over pretty quickly, but one factor that I was not aware of was, did anyone apart from myself and the BNP; know that they had 'Smith'? His henchmen had been to tell me but do the authorities know?

    I moved along the back of the building and there were four windows none of which were lit. I examined each window and could make nothing out. Back to the door and I risked easing it open so that I could see along the corridor. I held my breath because not ten feet from me there was a soldier sitting on a chair outside the nearest room. Fortunately, for me, his chin was down on his chest, which rose and fell gently, indicating that he was dozing. I slipped inside the door walked up to the soldier and hit him with the butt of the Glock. I propped him on his chair, took his keys opened the door and went into the room. 'Smith' was tied to a chair with his back to the door.

He started to speak but I stayed right behind him so he couldn't see me. I took out my Glock knife. It seemed to me that this would be less traceable and quieter. I put my hand over his mouth and slipped the knife between his ribs twice, first into the right lung and then the left. 'Smith' died quietly. The action I had taken ensured no noise, not much blood and a quick passing! I left the room, locked up, returned the keys to the guard, and left the way I had come.

I was back in the car in my normal clothes and had returned to the apartment within an hour after having completed a very successful trip! I wondered how the BNP would respond. It was out of my hands now anyway. When I got into my half of the flat, that was the original apartment, it was empty! There was a message on my spare mobile from Sumisu, *'We will be in touch. Contact minimum!'*

So they'd both gone. Bill, Stacey and Ethan had finished for the day so I really was alone and it was blissfully quiet. I went into my lounge with the coffee I had just made, poured myself an Oban, turned on some soothing music and sat in my high-backed, leather rocking chair closing my eyes. I reflected on the night's actions. How much had what I'd done been for the good of the cause, and how much for my own satisfaction? Was I no more than a cold-blooded killer? Was there another way to bring the action to a satisfactory conclusion?

The facts were fairly straightforward. 'Smith' was a violent thug who had jeopardised the success of the mission and he would have ended up in prison or hurting someone himself, if he hadn't done so earlier in his life. He was in it for the violence and so in my book deserved a violent end. The fact that I'm thinking this way was testimony that I wasn't deriving personal satisfaction. Looking for alternatives was not an option because of the time available and the risk that 'Smith' may have blown the gaff on me and the overall plan. It was my hope that the BNP were going to create a storm because I felt sure that the Americans would lose the body! I just hoped that the BNP had the wit to photograph 'Smith' when he was taken.

Chapter 16

Reflecting on where we have come to over the last few weeks was a mental exercise that I wasn't usually into but then my 'usual' work is much more like the 'Smith' thing and that was over and done with in a moment. What I have been doing was more of a long-term project by comparison. Also it came from within me, not instructed by some outside agency or the Gurentai and that was something to deal with. So what have I achieved?

At the moment we have the PM jetting off to the US to arse-lick round Obama. The French and the Germans have been talking to our military about joint projects to build aircraft carriers, jets and tanks. UKIP was like a dog chasing its tail, they're pleased to have the extra public support but have reservations about the European connection. What could happen is that when the electoral system changes, as I've no doubt it will, UKIP will undoubtedly have a number of fully-fledged members of parliament. They are exceptionally excited about that and it outweighs any reservations that they may have held. The BNP have been at the centre of some troubling allegations, (what's new?) surrounding the violence outside certain RAF bases and they are making a great noise about a missing member.

At home the newspapers, TV and Radio bulletins are talking about the 'special relationship' almost daily. The Breakfast Shows are analysing the history of the term and also interviewing foreign correspondents about the long-term effects of a cooling of the Trans-Atlantic relationship. There is a strengthening of opinion that we need to review the balance of the links that we have with the US and the more outspoken experts were stating that all we are doing is redressing that balance, which had been tipped over to the US side without the successive governments of the UK, since the 2nd World War, doing anything to maintain a suitable agreement between the two countries. Perhaps all that I had done was spurred the sleeping giant, that is the British Government, into action.

The government were also saying that they had planned to close some of the unnecessary US bases and to ensure that we have control over the remaining sites. They were also being renamed as USAF rather than RAF. When all is said and done they are guests on our shores. It was rumoured in the media that we were to demand an apology for the actions of the CIA in Bells Hill in Scotland. I feel certain that it will not end the CIA's involvement in the UK they will just have to be more careful in the future. The only reason they were discovered was because we were actively involved in actions against the States.

The other things with regards to our culture will be slower to evolve and change so the work is not over and there will always be a need to maintain our Englishness. The closer relationship with the European countries is also important in that it must be managed in a way that is less like the manner in which we have not managed the US. The French were very cautious with us in the post war period and into the 1960s and 70s, and that is the way we need to be with them in their turn and also with America.

The relationship with the European Economic Community is there and may have to be maintained for trade and mutual support but France and Germany are our nearest neighbours and we need to develop the trust between us. The military cooperation was a very good beginning!

    I still had heard nothing from Naomi and Sumisu san, which was slightly worrying. I had all this good news and no one to share it with. Had the CIA or someone else discovered them? What was disturbing most of all was the possibility that they had severed all contact to protect themselves and me from discovery? I tried texting on the new phone to their new devices. I waited but there was no reply. I didn't know what to do. For the first time in many months I was at a loss! My mentor that had moved me on in my thinking and skills and my companion that I had fought with and loved were out of contact and I was sure for very good reasons. What else could I do but revert to my 'normal' existence.

    I went for a run ending at the annexe and then spent an hour in the gym before warming down on the dojo. I showered and walked on to the local for a pint with the lads!

Chapter 17

It was almost a week since I'd parted with Naomi and Sumisu and still there had been no word from them. I had only tried to contact them the once, I thought discretion was of prime importance for all our sakes. My routine had returned to something like normal with me spending time training and handling the one or two accounts that I looked after. In the apartment things were moving quite nicely with Bill and Ethan overseeing the work. All the major restructuring, removing walls and partitioning that was necessary, had been complete. It was now a case of decoration, furnishing and finishing off. That can take an age at times.

Ethan was doing very well, which was hardly surprising as the working conditions were as good as the pay. He'd also started driving lessons! I think he had an eye on the Jag, kept talking about chauffeuring and is also a bit of a star pupil for Vince Thompson having taken part in his first Aikido competition with a top three finish. We'd started to do a bit of sparring under the watchful eye of Vince. I could see that the lad would want more involvement in the future. My feeling is that we need to get him some qualifications other than the violent kind! I wondered, privately whether he would be capable of accountancy or book keeping. Perhaps that was merely because of my expertise.

Bill and Stacey were like gold for me. They run the apartment and annexe brilliantly. They actually haven't brought up my 'Robin Hood' activities although I've not encouraged any conversations along those lines. Stacey was curious about the whereabouts of Naomi. They seem to have hit it off quite well.

    I've checked my accounts and they continue to grow, taking all my assets into consideration, on paper I was now a millionaire! The house in France would be great if I could get to it! That was something that would need to be looked into because there was little point in it if it wasn't going to be used. Although at the moment it was a liability and therefore tax deductible! Being an accountant I was scrupulous with my records, mostly! I was aware that I had to ensure all my dealings were transparent so that no official had any reason to investigate my business. This was all just as well because of a visitor I received a couple of days later. I'd just got back from a run when there was a knock at the door of my apartment. Stacey answered, as I was just getting out of the shower. When I got into my lounge there were two people there,

"Good morning," I smiled.

"Patrick, this is Detective Inspector Kathryn Best and Sergeant Gerald Maltby," Stacey stated in a very formal way with a blush!

    I walked across to the two police personnel and shook hands and asked if they would like a drink. They both declined but I asked Stacey if she would make me a coffee. My mind was a whirl of confused thoughts and the adrenaline had begun to flow.

"What can I do for you Inspector?" I asked looking her straight in the eyes.

She was tall, about 5' 10", slim and had the most striking grey eyes. She was wearing a light grey business suit with shiny black shoes and had the most disarming smile. However, there was something steely in her gaze, which was borne out in the way she spoke.

"Mr Steele, do you mind if I call you Patrick?" I shook my head and she went on, "Patrick I have a few questions about your whereabouts and movements over the last two or three weeks."

"Ok Inspector, carry on!" I said.

"Can you tell me where you have been since November 27th?" she demanded.

"Of course I can Inspector Best," I responded.

The next ten minutes were spent with me detailing where I'd been and what I'd done. I always had communications with my clients and when I visited a place I had not been too previously I set up meetings to 'sell my wares' so that I had reason to be where I was. I supplied the Inspector with dates and times of meetings and contact details. All the time I talked the Sergeant took notes and Kathryn Best watched me like a hawk. I maintained eye contact and channelled my thoughts as taught in Aikido. When I had gone through the mechanics of my movements she thanked me and went on,

"Patrick you have been very helpful but aren't you interested in why we want to know?" she said slightly sarcastically.

"Of course Inspector Best it has been in my mind since I walked in and saw you two sitting here but I just thought we would get to that when the basics of what you required had been completed. So why are you here?" I demanded.

She smiled, raised her very finely trimmed eyebrows and looked down at the notepad she had opened on her lap.

"Patrick as I understand it you are accomplished in Aikido, is that so?"

"Yes I suppose, although I have no qualifications. I use the art as a method of personal training and self-discipline," I replied.

"Are you a member of a club Patrick?" she went on.

"Yes I go to the local one and my sensei," she raised her eyebrows again, "Teacher, is Vince Thompson. He thinks I could be a black belt but I don't have time to compete," I responded.

"Patrick how on earth do you maintain this luxurious lifestyle you follow?" she asked disbelievingly.

"Inspector I have been very fortunate in the last three years to have been taken on by a number of high value clients. One in particular, based in Japan, has been exceedingly generous, but as you will see from my diary, is very demanding of my time," I explained. "In fact the reason I have been to see a few of my clients recently was to tell them to look elsewhere for an accountant as I am unable to continue with their business.

My Japanese employer has required that I travel to his country on a more regular basis. While I am young enough I am greedy enough to want to feather my own nest!" I grimaced.

"Ok Patrick. One other thing! Have you any weapons training at all?" she glared at me full on.

There it was. The trick question thrown in at the end of the interview! The question for me was how to respond and the obvious was to avoid lying because this was one smart lady and I would lay odds on that she knew the answer already!

"At University I was into OTC and Bodyguard school. It involved rifle shooting and unarmed combat," I explained. "It was an obvious course to follow for us testosterone pumping young men in our formative years.

"Why the bodyguard school Patrick?" she asked gently.

"It was the next level and anyway it only lasted a month or so!" I countered.

"Have you ever put any of the skills to the test?" she went on.

"No! I am an accountant Inspector! I wrestle with figures," I countered.

"Thanks for your time Patrick," She smiled as she rose gracefully from the sofa. "If we have any further questions we will get back to you!" she left that statement hanging in the air as she left the apartment. I let Stacey show them out. Just as they reached the door she turned,

"If you intend going abroad Patrick would you mind letting me know?" she smiled sweetly, like the Cheshire cat! She also held out a business card. I took the card and looked at her and replied,

"Is this because you want to come with me? I do have a mini chateau in France that needs my attention!" I said waving her business card.

She blushed slightly and left. I laughed and got a slap from Stacey for my trouble.

"You want to be careful of her Patrick she is clever, that one!" Stacey added.

"Yes, but I have nothing to reproach myself for!" I responded.

"Patrick I do not know, and don't want to know what you get up to but you and your two Japanese friends are more than accountants and business people!" with that Stacey sniffed and turned stalking back into the kitchen where I could hear her banging pots and pans around.

Thinking about what Stacey had said filled me with questions about where my 'career' would take me in years to come. Killing people has its risks! I was also wondering why the police had come calling in the first place. The only answer I could come up with was the BNP! I may be a mile away in my thinking but they were the group who had most to complain about since I wasted 'Smith'. I wouldn't put it passed them to have given my surname to plod!

    I continued my routine for the day but felt unsettled and was relieved when I received a text on my business phone ***'Hotel 19:00 today'*** Okay there were only two people that had that number so what could Sumisu or Naomi want? The remainder of the day was spent in a state of nervous tension that meant any task was not completed effectively. I'd been stomping around for the afternoon when I realised that I wasn't using the skills that I had learned in Aikido. I sat down and spent fifteen minutes breathing and internalising my thoughts, assessing my body and flexing as many groups of muscles as I could. I then showered, changed and set off to the hotel. I knew which hotel because we had only used one in close proximity to the apartment. I arrived at 18:45 and ordered coffee and sat at a table in a corner where I could observe the space. I watched comings and goings but also I checked out all the people sat at tables drinking, reading and chatting. I was looking for singletons, people who looked 'professional' and who were doing what I was doing. I didn't spot anyone.

Sumisu materialised next to me.

"Good evening Patrick san," he said quietly signalling me not to get up.
"I do not want to draw attention to ourselves," he concluded.

I nodded and said,

"That seems sensible Sumisu san. How are you?"

Sumisu pondered my words for a little while and replied with,

"I am fine thank you Patrick. My reason for contacting you is to bring you up-to-date with what has been happening."

"That is much appreciated Sumisu san," I said responding politely.

"You were quite correct about how the CIA got on to us. It was the use of mobiles in the US and then later back in England. My phone was in use more than Naomi's and yours because I was in contact with my controllers in Japan. By replacing the phone the contact was broken. Of the three of us Naomi is the one who is completely in the clear. I understand you have had a visitor today Patrick!" he stated.

"How....!" I began, then paused and smiled, "Yes, Inspector Best and Sergeant Maltby!"

"Who do you think has given them your ID Patrick?" he asked.

"I'm guessing BNP Sumisu san. They will be annoyed that 'Smith' was killed and they will assume it was me and not the Yanks. I'm assuming that they have done no more because their leader has disappeared and without a body they have no proof of anything." I continued, "The police were satisfied with my movements because of the contacts I gave them but they will be on my back unless everything returns to normal for a while."

"We are all going to have to be very quiet for some time I believe Patrick. That is one of the reasons that Naomi Kobayashi is not with me this evening. We have decided that she needs to return to her base for a while rather than for us to be seen together. As you have never been privilege to where that is then she is safe," he ended.

"I understand Sumisu san. Does that mean that we will not be working together again as a unit?" I asked quietly dreading his response.

"Not at all Patrick but we will not meet at your place; we need to protect you also!" he responded. "We will contact in the way I have done today and I would suggest we change our business phones after each operation."

Everything that my mentor had said made sense and although I was disappointed not to see Naomi I think she had been aware of the difficulty of our situation before we had parted after Harrogate. I didn't want to find her with a bullet through her head as I had Misaki!

"Finally Patrick, you are to be congratulated on the success of this exercise that you in fact masterminded. We have achieved a great deal more than I thought possible. In fact I was quite sceptical in the beginning. The Gurentai are also very pleased that the focus on the US has been somewhat diluted. There has been some reaction in my own country and people have followed the political ramifications carefully!" he finished.

I pondered on his words for a long time. The Gurentai would use me again as would one or two of my former employers, but more than likely with short-term single jobs as before. The last two assignments had been spectacular by comparison! My account in Switzerland was doing very well even though this last job had cost me, rather than pulling in loads of revenue but I still had my monthly Japanese retainer, and although it's not professional footballer money £50000 a dozen times a year will keep the wolf from the door!

We took our leave of each other and I watched the erect back of the small but amazingly powerful man who had led me this far on my current path stride away through the busy foyer and I considered what my next steps would be.

Initially I returned home! I decided I would go for a few pints with my friends and re-establish myself in that group. Jet-setting all over the world as they saw it did nothing to maintain any kind of relationships.

Walking home from the pub was still not pleasurable; the beer aside it was still the same rubbish in the streets. It was almost impossible to put a foot down without stepping on or kicking some detritus from a fast food shop or coffee emporium. I suppose that was as much about the way we teach our children to clear up after themselves as it is on the way that food was presented for purchase. Much of this, of course was not biodegradable and firms based in the USA sponsor all of it and there of course was the root of the problems that we still have.

Strange how beer makes you happy some times and other evenings morbid! I was tending more to the latter as I left the pub. The litter was still there and it was still the same type so what had the last month or so been about? Well I suppose the change in culture would be slower and subtler. It would take generations to alter the behaviours of the young. At least the political situation was moving more rapidly. Why did I feel so low when everything had worked out so well? That's life I suppose!

On the plus side Bill, Stacey and now Ethan as well, were on side with regards to my extra-curricular activities. They haven't been given specifics about actual things that I had done and people I'd killed but they did know that what I do is confidential and they assume legal! They're also aware that I had improved situations for people. I would be surprised if Bill was unaware of some of the methods I'd used as he knows what weapons I have! To a degree they are all complicit in the sort of work in which I'm involved and in the near future they will need a pay rise. I've also broached the subject of qualifications for Ethan with all three. Judging by the lad's response it was a case of some falling on stony ground but he was taking driving lessons! It'll be interesting to see how that develops.

I was sitting in my lounge and noticed a business card on the coffee table. I went across and picked it up and looked at it. It was the one given to me by Detective Inspector Kathryn Best! I looked at the number and pondered what I was going to do! She is a very attractive proposition.

"Forgive me Naomi…," I muttered as I dialled the number."